HOW NOT
TO BE
WEIRD

Also by Dawn McNiff

Little Celeste
Worry Magic

HOW NOT TO BE WEIRD

DAWN McNIFF

PRESS

First published in Great Britain in 2016 by
PICCADILLY PRESS
80–81 Wimpole St, London W1G 9RE
www.piccadillypress.co.uk

A CIP catalogue record for this book is available from the British
Library.

ISBN: 978-1-4714-0373-6
also available as an ebook

1

Printed and bound by Clays Ltd, St Ives Plc

Piccadilly Press is an imprint of Bonnier Publishing Fiction,
a Bonnier Publishing company
www.bonnierpublishingfiction.co.uk
www.bonnierpublishing.co.uk

For my best Gooner x

Chapter 1

There I was again.

Being the biggest loser ever.

Lying on my face on someone else's lawn, hiding.

I could hear the girls' footsteps coming along the pavement. Music from a phone, giggling and stuff.

Della and Casey.

I'd know their voices anywhere: they'd been in my class since I was five. They were second cousins – and real bully-girls.

I rolled over and jammed myself right under

the hedge, making sure my big feet weren't sticking out. Please, people whose garden this is – *don't* look out of your lounge window now.

'Weirdy, where are yoooooou?' the girls were crowing.

Ugh, Weirdy. They *always* called me that instead of Woody, which was my actual name.

'Weirdyyyyyyyy?'

Della's voice. She'd started the whole Weirdy thing, and Casey had copied her. Della was the brains; Casey was just the muscle.

The girls were cackling louder now, like they'd never had such fun. Or not since the last time they chased me, and I'd hidden behind those prams outside playgroup.

'Weirdy wuss? Boo hoo hooooo!' Yep, and sometimes, just for extra mean-ness, they called me Weirdy the Wuss too, cos they said I was a massive cry baby as well as weird. That started back in Year Four after I'd cried in assembly when the class stick insect died.

I loved that stick insect . . .

And I just couldn't help getting upset about

things. Mum said it was my star sign – my moon in Pisces making me too sensitive for my own good, or something.

Probably was true.

Like now . . . I really wanted to cry A LOT. I bit my lip hard.

The girls were getting closer. My heart started booming so loudly I was sure they'd hear it.

'Eww, look – that fat dog's eating those mouldy chips!'

They sniggered.

'Hey, wait – isn't that *Weirdy's* dog?' said Della.

GOONER?! Oh no, maybe he'd got out of the garden again and followed me? He was always doing that. He could unhook the latch with his nose, too, if people forgot to bolt it. If he got a sniff of me, he'd come and stare under the hedge and wag his tail like he'd won a fun hide-and-seek game. He'd so give away my hiding place . . .

The girls had stopped right by me.

I held my breath. I could see their feet through

the leaves. White and silver trainers. They seemed to be wearing exactly the same shoes. One of them stepped a millimetre away from my face, and stood on tiptoes, peering over into the garden.

A twig was sticking right up my nose, but I didn't dare move.

'Nah, he's nowhere. Looks like he's wussed off,' said Della. 'Even his rank dog didn't want to hang around with him.'

And then they tramped on past, down the street, laughing.

I let out my breath in a big puff.

Phew, they'd gone.

This time . . .

But what was I going to do when school started again? Stay in the bushes all day?

Lucky for me, Della was off to the other secondary school in town – but Casey was going to the same one as me.

School WITH Casey . . .

And WITHOUT Lu.

It was basically a humongous disaster.

Lu was my neighbour and very best friend, and Della and Casey left me alone A BIT more when I was with her, cos Lu could be pretty fierce. But she was in the year below, so she wasn't coming up to secondary with me.

I was going to be *worm food.*

It was raining now, and under the hedge it smelt of cat wee and mouldy leaves. But I stayed where I was, listening until the girls' voices got fainter. They were still going on and on:

'Weirdy? We just wanted to see your lovely, granny jumper.'

WHAT? My jumper wasn't for grannies!

Was it?

I sighed.

Mum'd bought it for me – from a charity shop – so it was bound to be true. This kind of thing had happened to me before, way *too* many times. Like when she bought me that wool cloak thing in Year Three, and everyone called me Fairy Godmother.

Why did I let Mum choose things for me? I mean, I had NO idea about fashion stuff, but

Mum wore ridiculous rainbowy sacks instead of clothes, and shouldn't be let loose in a shop by herself.

Oh God, my life . . .

It was raining hard now, and the girls had definitely gone. So I rolled out on to the lawn and scooted back on to the pavement, double-quick.

No sign of Gooner. Maybe Della had made a mistake, then . . .

Great, and look – I was CAKED in mud.

And I was going to be late for Nan. *And* I'd lain on the flowers I'd bought her from the garage – they were all squashed and had blobs of mud stuck to them.

I hoped Nan wouldn't be cross with me. She was my dad's mum, but I hadn't seen her since I was a baby, cos she fell out with Mum after my dad died. Then out of the blue last week, she'd sent me a card, inviting me for tea.

So I was going . . . but I was a gigantic bag of nerves.

I mean, I had no idea what to expect. Mum'd

hardly ever talked about Nan or my dad – and never anything good – so I'd sort of stored them at the back of my brain on a high shelf, out the way.

Until now.

I rubbed my face, feeling really flustered, and tried to straighten out the flowers, but it wasn't working at all.

Some older boys were coming along the road towards me, so I quickly started walking, trying to be casual. But I suddenly felt extra-shy – even more than usual cos of my jumper. I wondered if I had time to take it off, but then I thought that might make them notice me more. So I kept going, head down, staring at the pavement.

As they got closer, I felt like I'd forgotten how to walk normally. I didn't know how to hold my arms, and I went all stiff, awkward and lolloppy. I was so sure they were going to laugh at me.

I squashed myself close to the fence as I passed them, nearly tripping over my own feet and a small twig. But they took no notice of me at all – it was like I was invisible. Good . . .

As soon as they'd gone past, I pulled the jumper off over my head. At least my T-shirt was normal. Ish. It was made of organic hemp, but nobody would know.

I'd have to leg it now. Nan lived right across town.

The drizzle blew in my face as I ran. I hoped it was washing some of the mud off my face.

I just didn't know HOW I got myself into these messes . . .

I really had to do something about my *extreme* weirdness.

Starting right NOW, so I wouldn't be random and awkward at Nan's. And definitely before term started on Tuesday, or I'd stand out like a sore thumb and never make any friends. I had to get un-weird . . . and fast.

Maybe even make myself some un-weirding *rules*.

Yes . . .

Like:

Don't roll about under other people's hedges.

And:

Don't wear old lady clothes.

Duh.

Chapter 2

I hadn't got far when there was a loud toot-
tooting behind me.

I knew who it was without even turning
round.

Mum.

Being her usual embarrassing self.

Oh.

No.

Cringe . . .

I just kept jogging through the rain, pretending
not to hear her – even though the whole of
Europe must've heard.

TOOT!

Please just GO away, Mum, with your squeaky-toy hooter. Everything about her van was dumb.

She'd bought it in the summer for her job as a children's entertainer. She did these shows at kiddies' parties and called herself the Story Sheep. She'd hand-painted the van bright green with wonky flowers and *STORY SHEEP PARTIES – BAAAAAAAA!* in huge blobby letters down the side. Even *worse*, she usually drove it around *dressed* as a sheep too.

Death-by-Mum-embarrassment.

She wasn't giving up with her tooting. Of course not. She'd moved on to a full TUNE now.

Toot-toot-toot!

'WOODS!? IT'S MEEEEE!' she bellowed, drawing up next to me and winding down the van window. Course I *had* to turn round then.

She had her big woolly hood pulled up, and her nose was painted black around her nose ring.

Un-weirding rule – Keep away from mothers dressed as farm animals.

'Oh yeah, hi Mum,' I muttered.

'Wakey, wakey! You're such a daydreamer!' Her floppy ears bounced impatiently. 'I was calling you cos I just saw Gooner. Isn't he supposed to be with you?'

Gooner?

I turned and whistled.

There was a clatter and he came bombing out of a side street in a mad, clumsy gallop. A great big black blur of fur. Like a baby bear crossed with a Womble.

He skidded and threw himself at me, wiping his great, mucky paws on my T-shirt.

Great. Now THAT was dirty too.

I pushed him down. He cocked his head to one side and tried his puppy face, wagging hard, but I scowled.

'So it WAS you Della saw! What are you doing out of the garden? You're very bad.' I was trying to be cross with him, but it was always hard.

He was the best dog in the entire world. As well as the rudest and stinkiest.

He wagged harder – like he was dead pleased with himself.

And how had he got so soggy and brown? He literally looked like he'd been lying in some cow pats. But then I did too.

'So you off to Nan's?' said Mum. She knew I was. 'Do you want a lift? I've just finished my party, so I can drop you off.'

The rain was getting harder, but I shook my head.

'No, ta. 'S okay. I wanna walk.'

'Don't be daft, Woods – look at that cloud. It's going to pour down any minute.'

But I shook my head again. I was normally rubbish at arguing with Mum. She was SO bossy that I usually gave in for a quiet life. But I didn't want to get spotted in the sheep van by Della and Casey.

Just no.

'It's fine, Mum – I'm nearly there. See you later, yeah?' Anyway I knew she only wanted to give me a lift so she could be nosey and spy on Nan to see what she looked like these days.

'Oh well, okay, suit yourself,' said Mum. 'Gooner can stay with you. Say hi to Barbie for me.' And she drove off with a half-wave.

What? Take Gooner to *Nan's*? What if he was naughty? Not even if . . . WHEN.

Mum'd done that *on purpose*! Just cos she was miffed that Nan hadn't invited her as well. When I'd got the card from Nan she'd got all suspicious, too – like, *what does SHE want?* – and eye-rolly, cos Nan had called me *'Dear William'*.

William was my first name – same as my dad's – but Mum'd always called me Woody, my middle name. I actually liked William better cos it was more *normal*, but Mum didn't like normal stuff – she was allergic to it.

Gooner had wandered off into a garden. I rushed in after him and pulled him out by his scruff.

Yeah, thanks Mum – I didn't even have a lead.

And I had no time to take him home now. I

had to take him to Nan's with me, make him be good – and just pray he didn't gas us with one of his empty-the-room farts.

I took some deep breaths. Today was really not going my way.

Chapter 3

Number four, Toadpool Road. Blue door.

Nan's house.

The garden was all neat, and the grass looked like a golf lawn. Not like ours with all Mum's scruffy vegetables, falling-down sheds, and things planted in old tyres.

I made Gooner sit, using my jumper as a kind of lead. Then I knocked gently.

A lady opened the door so quickly that it made me jump.

Was she Nan? She was old, but she didn't look like other people's grandmas. She had long, blonde hair and girly sort of clothes. I looked more granny-ish than her.

I looked at the number on the door again. No, this was definitely the right house.

'Er . . . hi,' I said, shuffling my feet.

If this *was* Nan, then I suddenly got why Mum had called her Barbie instead of her real name Barbara. She really was more like a Barbie doll than a normal Nan.

She didn't say hi back. She was looking at my wet, muddy T-shirt, and half-frowning as if she didn't like me already. As if I was a robber or something.

'Nan, it's . . . er . . . me, Woody,' I said quickly, feeling my face turning pink. 'I mean . . . you know . . . *William*, your grandson.' I tried to brush the mud off my T-shirt, but I just smeared it.

'Oh, William!' She looked right at me and smiled then. She had some lipstick on her teeth. '*Of course* it's you. Sorry . . . babe.'

Babe? She sounded like a teenager.

'Oh, but you're so tall now! I was expecting someone so much smaller.'

It was true – I was tall for my age. Skinny and gangly with massive feet. I hated being tall, especially when my head stuck up above everyone in assembly. I always bent my knees and sunk down lower so that I wouldn't show up so much.

I handed Nan the squashed flowers. 'Sorry about them . . . I . . . er . . . fell over.'

I felt my cheeks go pinker as I lied. But I couldn't exactly tell her that I'd been hiding from Della and Casey under a hedge.

'Come in out of the rain. You're getting soaked to the skin,' she said. She had a soft voice, and an accent like those Essex people off that programme Lu's mum watched.

As I stepped onto the mat, Gooner yanked away from me, and barged past my legs into the hall. He wagged his tail at Nan, whacking a tall lamp in the hall. The lamp wobbled, but I bounded forward and caught it just before it fell.

'Sorry,' I mumbled. 'Er . . . I had to bring my dog. Well, he kind of followed me by . . . er . . . mistake.'

I wished I could stop saying 'er', but I always said it when I was embarrassed. Stupid me.

Nan gave Gooner a look, and I could tell it wasn't love at first sight. Her house was definitely much too white to have a Gooner in it.

Gooner tried his cute-puppy look on her, his head on one side. But then he ruined it by shaking himself hard and spraying her with watery mud, polka-dotting her white jeans and cream door curtain.

'NO, Gooner!' I cried. 'Oh no, sorry. Maybe I should just leave him outside? Except I don't have a lead to tie him up, so he'll probably run away and raid your bin . . .'

I glanced up at her face. Was she cross?

'Sorry,' I muttered again.

'No, no, you're all right, babe. He can come in,' said Nan, in a too-bright voice. 'But he'll have to lie on a towel,' she added, firmly. I could tell she secretly thought Gooner was a dirty hog-dog, but she was trying hard to be nice.

While I took off my shoes, she opened the loo door and pulled some pale pink, fluffy towels out of a cupboard. She spread one towel on her smart sofa for me to sit on, and one on her cream carpet for Gooner.

Gooner looked at the perfect towel and then at me – like he thought it was all a bad joke. I pointed at it and told him to lie down, but he didn't move. He'd turn into a performing circus dog for a gravy-bone biscuit, but he never did as he was told for *free* – he expected to be paid in snacks. He was so *awkward* like that.

I shoved him down.

'Stay,' I said fiercely, and gave him a proper stern look.

Un-weirding rule – Don't go round with doggy weirdos.

'Great. Now, I've got us some treats. I'll just pop and get them,' said Nan, smiling, and went off to the kitchen.

I sat on the edge of the sofa on my towel, looking around. Nan's house was smart – and very tidy and *normal*. It was the kind of house that wouldn't be cringey to invite friends to. Not like our upside-down house which was a mad muddle of strange, hippy things like crystals, hammocks and goddess statues; and racks of Mum's old sheep costumes, which stunk cos she'd made them herself from real sheep fleece.

I could tell that Nan would never dress as a dumb sheep . . . not ever.

Nan came out with a neat tray of cookies, glasses of fizzy apple juice, and some pink napkins with little flowers on. Oh, and they were my favourite double-chocolate, toffee cookies. The kind I always tried to swap with Lu for my carrot sticks or yoghurt raisins at school. I wasn't allowed them at home, because Mum said they had hydrogenated fat in them, which was bad fat that made you die early.

I put a cookie on my plate. And then another.

Nan sat down next to me, gripping a glass of juice. Her nails were purply-red with little jewels on. Mum's nails were purple sometimes too, but only when she'd peeled loads of beetroot for making wine. Really, I understood now why Mum and Nan didn't get on.

'Thanks . . . er . . . Nan,' I said. It felt weird calling her Nan, because she was a stranger and people were supposed to know their nans.

'Oh no, please don't call me Nan or Gran, or anything like that,' she said. She giggled and batted the air. 'Crumbs, you'll make me feel so old! I'd rather be a glamMA than a grandma!'

I nodded slowly, but I had no idea what she was on about. A glamMA? What was that?

'You know, a glamorous grandma?' She giggled. 'Oh never mind – maybe just call me Babs, like my friends do.'

'Okay.' I nodded again, but I was still lost.

'So-o-o, here you are.' She patted my arm and looked at me hard, like she was inspecting me. She had long eyelashes with thick black make-up on them. They looked like spiders' legs. I felt my cheeks heat up again and I didn't know where to look. So I just bit my cookie and stared down at Gooner. He'd already made a brown, smeary mark on his towel.

'So, I expect you were a bit surprised to hear from me after so long?' she said. And without waiting for my answer: 'But I just thought it was about time that we got to know each other now you're nearly twelve . . . and you can come without your mum.' She said *your mum* a bit snippily. 'After all, you are my only grandchild.'

She was still looking at me. I wondered if I had mud in my ears. Or maybe Marmite on my nose. I fidgeted in my seat, and stared at my socks. Mum had knitted them, but they'd gone a bit wrong – they were like loose, woolly bags on my feet.

'You look *so* much like my Will when he was young . . .' she said finally. 'You're really like two peas in a pod.'

'Erm, yeah,' I nodded, nudging Gooner with my foot. He'd started licking his bottom noisily.

But actually I didn't know if I was like my dad or not. He'd died in an accident before I was two, and I'd only ever seen one photo of him. A blurry one of him as a teenager in one of Mum's old class photos from school – and you couldn't even see his face properly. He and Mum had split up when I was born, so she probably threw all the other pictures of him away when he left.

'Have you got any photos of my dad?' I blurted.

Then my face burned up. My blabber mouth! I shouldn't have said that. What if she got upset? People get sad looking at pictures of dead people. It was just that, all of a sudden, I really, *really* wanted to see my dad.

But Nan beamed.

'Oh yes, of course, sweetheart!' she said. 'Yes, yes, I've got tonnes!'

She jumped up and pulled a thick, white photo album of the shelf. She sat down right next to me, and opened it in the middle. Her hands were shaking a bit, making her golden bracelets jangle.

'This is him when he was about thirteen,' she said softly, pointing with her long nail at a smiley boy.

And there he was.

Staring back at me, close up.

Light brown hair; blue eyes.

She quietly turned the page, pointing at other photos.

A boy on a bike. A boy with a big brown dog . . .

I sort of shuddered and hoped Nan didn't notice. But this was freaky. Because even I could see that he looked like me. Or rather, I looked like him.

Except he was me on a very, very good day. Like a new, improved me. Cooler and . . . un-weirder. By miles.

Nan got out more albums. She had piles of them.

Another photo of him wearing his school uniform.

The uniform for Hawthorn Secondary. My dad and mum had both gone there – it was where they'd met. And it was where I was going too, in just a few days when term started – bad luck for me.

'That was his very first day at Hawthorn,' said Nan.

He was smiling into the camera. He looked confident – not a jibbering wreck like I was going to be on my first morning.

Nan seemed to be lost in the photos, turning the pages slowly and smiling.

There were lots of pictures of him laughing with his mates.

'He's got such smashing friends,' Nan said. *Has?*

It was like she'd forgotten for a minute that he'd died.

She was gazing down at the same page in a dream.

'And quite a way with the girls too,' she said, with a sad laugh.

Huh, I had a way with girls too. A way of making them bully me under hedges.

She turned a page.

Photos of Dad in a band.

Cuttings from the local paper of him in a play.

Crikes, he looked like the coolest boy in the school.

Why couldn't I have taken after him instead of being weird like Mum? It was so UNFAIR!

Nan must've read my mind.

'Yes . . .' She laughed softly. 'He really was my Golden Boy.'

Then she did a funny, tight smile so her lipsticky lips uncrinkled and went red and smooth.

'Come on, babe – I'll show you his room.'

Chapter 4

I followed her to the stairs.

Gooner leapt to his feet too, wagging his tail hard.

'NO, stay!' I said, wagging my finger at him. He sort of humphed and flopped down on his fat belly again.

Nan led me upstairs and into a bedroom.

'This is his room,' she said in a half-whisper. 'Just like it was when he left for the States – exactly ten years ago last month. Have a look around.'

Look?! My eyes were nearly popping out.

The room was jammed with all my dad's real stuff.

From when he was alive.

A shivery tingle ran down me.

Wow.

It was like a My Dad Museum.

Posters of long-ago bands and girls.

Faded beer mats and concert tickets stuck to the wardrobe. And I could see through the glass doors that it was still full of men's clothes.

Nan sighed, clocking my look.

'Oh, I don't know why I keep it all – daft, really.' She did a high laugh. 'I guess I'm just a bit of a hoarder . . .'

There was a peeling motorbike sticker on the side of the wardrobe. That's how the accident had happened – on a bike.

I did another shiver, and moved away quickly – over to the chest of drawers, which had framed photos on top of it.

My dad on a sledge.

At a wedding, wearing a suit with a young-looking Nan.

My dad grinning his face off, holding a Rubik's Cube . . .

WHAT? No way!

I LOVED RUBIK'S CUBES TOO!

I had four of them, in different shapes – and I could do them in quick-fire time.

'Ha, that's a funny piccie,' Nan laughed, softly. 'He won a competition at school – fastest Rubik's cuber or something. Look at him, beaming.'

I didn't know why, but tears suddenly prickled in my eyes.

Maybe I *had* inherited something from Dad after all. Even if it was kind of a stupid thing.

I picked up the photo to have a closer look.

But Nan was reaching up to a shelf above my head. She brought down a posh glass display case.

I stared. Inside, lying on a small velvet cushion, was a tiny Rubik's Cube on a key-ring chain.

A perfect, golden, miniature cube.

'This,' said Nan, 'is your dad's special cube.'

She opened the case and handed the cube to me.

It was shiny, and all its squares were different shades of metal – golds, silvers and bronzes. And when I twisted it, it worked just like a bigger cube.

I'd never seen one like that before – not ever.

'Wow, this is so . . . cool,' I breathed.

'Yes, he thought so too,' smiled Nan. 'It was his most precious thing. He called it his "charm". He was a strange boy sometimes!'

'What d'you mean?'

'He had this nutty idea that the cube made him more popular and charming or something,' she said, shrugging. He always had it with him, at school and everywhere!'

Uh?

'So . . . he thought it had – what? *Powers?*' I asked.

This was getting a bit freaky.

'Oh yes, one hundred per cent convinced!' She shook her head and gazed down at her feet with a sad half-smile. 'He always was a superstitious kid. But then it's fair to say that he *was* a right little charmer – that much was true . . .

Awmygawd! *What* on earth was that?' Nan cried.

Something had gone crash downstairs.

Gooner!

I laid the cube back on its velvet cushion and flew down.

Gooner was sitting in the middle of the lounge, licking his lips. The coffee table was on its side. The juice was spilled on the carpet, and the cookies had all gone.

'What have you done?' I snapped. 'NO!'

He burped and wagged his tail. He had crumbs all round his face. 'Bad dog! I can't take you anywhere!' I hissed.

Gooner burped again. Even though I was worried about the mess, I was trying not to laugh. Mum's boyfriend Shaun said Gooner had 'comic timing' and should have his own comedy show on telly. I didn't agree with Shaun about much, but he was right on that.

Nan came hurrying in.

'Um, sorry, he scoffed the biscuits,' I said, blushing. 'I'll mop up the juice!' I glanced at her face. Would she tell me off?

Nan waved her hand through the air. 'Oh no, don't you worry – these things happen,' she said. But I saw her nose wrinkle a bit when she looked down at Gooner.

I didn't blame her.

'Well, er . . . I think I'd better take him home now,' I said, a bit flustered. 'But thanks for the biscuits and that.'

Nan smiled. 'Okay, babe – but you've gotta promise to come again, okay?'

I nodded, dragging Gooner out into the hall by his collar.

'Oh, and maybe you could give me your mobile number before you go,' Nan said, 'so I can text you?'

'Um, well, I don't have a mobile,' I said, shuffling into my trainers. Mum didn't agree with mobile phones for kids – she said they microwaved your head.

'You don't?' Nan tutted, like I'd said Mum didn't feed me or something. 'Well, then I'd like to buy you one! Or, in fact . . . WAIT right there,' she said.

I stood on the doormat while she rummaged in the hall drawer.

She handed me a mobile phone.

'There – have this. It's my old one. It still has some credit on it.'

This was her OLD one? But it was so posh.

'Oh,' I stammered. 'Er . . . wow, thanks!'

This was great! I'd been the only kid in Year Six without a phone. But I'd have to hide it – Mum would spit sheep fleece if she saw it.

'And . . .' she said, her eyes darting down again at my T-shirt, 'maybe I could treat you to some new clothes and things.'

Right. My clothes again. She and Della really could've started a We-Hate-Woody's-Stuff Club. 'What d'you say?' Nan went on. 'A fun shopping trip with my best grandson!' She clapped her hands. 'Oh, I'd LOVE that!'

I bit my lip, and sort of nodded and shook my head at the same time. It seemed ungrateful to say no, but I knew Mum'd have ten thousand kinds of fits if I went shopping with Nan. And shopping was not my favourite thing.

But Nan seemed to take my nod-shake as a yes. She patted my arm and beamed.

'Great. So shall we go to the mall tomorrow?' she asked. 'Before school starts. That's on Tuesday, isn't it?'

School . . . the day after tomorrow.

My belly rolled over. Don't remind me.

Hmmm . . . maybe some new clothes *would* help my un-weirding. Save me from going to school dressed like a boy that everyone wanted to bog-wash.

But still, shopping in a *mall*? It was like a nightmare come true.

'Um, thanks – but I'd better . . . er . . . like, check with Mum first. You know . . .'

Of course, there was no way I was ACTUALLY checking with Mum. I just needed to think about it.

'Okay, darling. Text me later to let me know then.' She wrote her number down on a pink heart-shaped Post-it note and gave it to me. 'Oh, it's been just so lovely to see you!'

She hugged me and then held me away from

her, staring at me hard again. 'And I still can't get over how much you look like my Will . . .' Her voice trailed off. 'Your dad would've been very proud of you, you know,' she said, softly.

I felt a lump in my throat then, and swallowed quickly. Because I really didn't think he would've been.

Gooner was scratching the paint on her door, asking to go out, so she pulled it open.

'Bye William, sweetheart!'

William again . . . It was going to take some getting used to.

She kissed me on the cheek, but missed. The kiss made a big buzz in my ear, so loud it hurt. I wanted to waggle my finger in my ear, but I thought it would be rude, like I was wiping her kiss off.

'Yeah, thanks. Bye, Nan . . . er . . . I mean Barbi . . . I mean Babs,' I said, dragging Gooner down the path. My head was spinning as I hurried away down the street.

Nan was still on the doorstep. Waving. Then she closed the door.

Just in time.

On the corner, Gooner made a loud burping sound and threw up all the cookies, mixed with all the chips he'd wolfed at the bus stop.

Ewww . . .

Un-weirding rule — Re-home Gooner.

Still, luckily the sick had gone in the gutter. Rather than on Nan's cream carpet.

I pulled him away before he could eat it, like he usually did.

'GOD, you are so *disgusting*. I think YOU need a make-you-charming charm.'

Whatever one of those actually was.

Strange . . . but also kind of *awesome*.

Awesome like my dad.

Chapter 5

I put Gooner on his granny-jumper lead again.

He was waddling slowly in a zig-zag, stopping to cock his leg on every bit of grass or litter. He always did about a thousand wees on a walk, but never seemed to run out. Shaun said he had a bladder like an elephant.

I was dawdling too, in a total daze. My head was full up with nans and dads . . .

Especially dads.

And it was odd, because as me and Gooner got back on the main road, there seemed to be dads *everywhere*. Maybe cos it was a

Sunday. Or maybe I just had dads on the brain.

A dad getting off a bus with two little children.

A dad driving a car full of kids, stopped at the lights. A dad pushing a pushchair towards the shops.

I wondered if my dad had ever taken ME on a bus, or pushed ME in a pushchair.

I guessed I'd never know. I wouldn't dare ask Nan in case it upset her. And I knew Mum'd only say, *Pah, him!* Just the mention of his name made her feel sick.

The little boy in the pushchair dropped his toy on the pavement. His dad picked it up and handed it back to him, doing a funny cartoon voice and making the boy giggle.

I wondered if my dad was funny. He looked like he was. He was smiling a lot in all those photos.

I wanted to follow the pushchair dad more. But I could see a group of kids up ahead eating chips outside the chip shop – so I pulled Gooner and whipped away down an alley. Just in case one of them was Della or Casey. Or Della-

Salmonella and Casey Rat-facey, as Lu called them.

We went the park way.

And that's when I thought of it – just by the park entrance.

My dad's grave was in the graveyard right next to the park.

Just through the metal curly gates.

I'd visited him before, but only once, a long time ago with Mum. I didn't even know why she'd taken me, and I hadn't been since. It hadn't even occurred to me to go – he'd just been this long-way-away dead person who had nothing to do with me. But now everything felt different.

My dad's actual grave . . .

Where he *was*.

My heart did a hiccup and I got goosebumps.

I didn't stop to think about it. I hurried across the road and through the gate. I couldn't remember exactly where the grave was, but I knew it had a white headstone.

It was only a small graveyard. I walked around, pulling Gooner on his jumper-lead behind me.

Then I saw it.

By the stone side wall. The headstone was so pure white it looked brand new. And it had perfect pink flowers arranged in a vase, and neat grass. Nan must have tidied it up every day – like her house.

I walked up to it slowly, tugging Gooner along next to me. Now I'd seen Nan's photos, I could imagine Dad's face.

I did a shiver. It felt like he was really near, but not in a spooky or creepy way. More like he was watching me from Heaven or something.

I stared at the writing on the stone.

William Trindle. Forever missed.

I was a Trindle too.

And a William.

William him . . . William me . . .

I crouched down in front of the grave, and traced the carved letters of his name.

'Hi Dad,' I whispered.

Chapter 6

We didn't stay long cos an old lady came along the path, and Gooner was pulling on his jumper-lead to go.

We scurried out and over the road to the park. Gooner's favourite place in the universe.

He stopped at the park entrance and refused to move – doing a lead protest like he always did when he wanted to be let off. So I let him go so he could have a good sniff-about.

I had to be careful where I was stepping as I walked – the path was covered in worms brought out by the rain. I kept stopping to rescue them, picking them up and carrying them gently to a bush where they were safe. I always did it cos I just couldn't stand thinking about them being stood on and squashed. I saved ladybirds, and even wasps too. When I was little, I wanted to be a bug vet when I grew up.

Oh. But I probably should do worm-rescuing on the quiet from now on. For un-weirding's sake.

'Hey, Gooner?!'

He was galloping off across the park.

'Gooner, get here!' I yelled, charging after him.

He ignored me and nipped through the open gate of the playground. He hopped over the bottom of the slide with his ears all pricked up, and poked his head into the toddler playhouse. His big, woolly bottom was sticking out the door, his tail wagging like mad.

I stomped towards him crossly.

But as I got closer, I heard a noise. Like a whimpery crying sort of noise. And it wasn't Gooner. His tail was still wagging.

Someone was in the toddler house.

I crouched down by the door. There was a

girl who looked about about my age in there, squashed onto one of the little low benches. She had a huge yellow waterproof on, with her hood pulled right up. Her arms were around Gooner's neck and her face was buried in his fur. She was rocking as she sobbed and sobbed.

I felt myself gulp – I always got sad when other people cried, even when I had no reason. In the Infants, I sometimes even used to cry when *other* children got told off.

I stood up and then crouched down again. I didn't know what to do. She hadn't noticed I was there yet. Maybe I should just creep away, in case she reckoned I was spying on her? But I couldn't take Gooner with me cos she was hugging him so tight.

Yuck, she was making a big mistake with that long hug – Gooner stank, and now she'd stink too.

Gooner glanced round at me and wagged his tail awkwardly. He liked making friends, but the look on his face said this was too much love all at once.

The girl put her head up then. Her face was red, wet and scrunched up. She saw me and jumped. She drew her head down inside her coat, like tortoises do into their shells, so I could only see her eyes.

'Er . . . hi . . . ' I said. 'My dog . . . he came to see you.'

I dropped my granny jumper in the dirt and then snatched it up again, trying to hide it from her behind my back, but flicked mud up my trouser leg instead.

So much coolness . . .

She nodded and shrank deeper into her coat. I didn't want to be rude or embarrass her by looking at her when she was crying so much, so I just stared down at Gooner's paws.

He still had his head on her lap. She was twisting his ears round and round. He was loving it and had gone into a sleepy daze. So I had to stay too, waiting, knelt down with the rain plopping on my back.

She was sniffing loads, and poking around in her pockets. I guessed she was looking for a tissue, so I pulled out the napkin Nan had given me for the cookies. Then I wished I hadn't. Oh no, she would think I was weird for having that. But she just grabbed it and blew her nose.

'Ta,' she said.

And then she just started talking and talking from inside her coat, like she couldn't stop.

She said they'd only just moved to town to a small flat, but the new landlord didn't allow pets, so they'd had to give away her cat, Pickle.

I didn't say much cos I couldn't think of anything to say, so I just nodded. But I felt so sorry for her. I'd HATE it if I had to give Gooner away – even though he was obviously the most annoying dog ever born.

'We just took him to his new home,' she gulped. 'The lady was really nice and everything – she said I can visit. But it's not the same – he won't be able to sleep on my bed any more!' she said with another sob.

'That's horrible, ' I said, my voice cracking. No, Woody, don't you start crying too! I coughed. 'Really horrible,' I said again, more firmly.

She nodded. 'Thanks.'

She rubbed her eyes with her fists.

'What's his name?' she asked.

'My dog? Oh, he's called Gooner,' I said. 'Because he's a clumsy, big goon . . . not because I'm an Arsenal fan or anything.'

'Uh?'

'Arsenal football fans are called Gooners,' I explained. 'So everyone always thinks I named him after them, but I don't like footie.' Another reason why I got left out at school. I just tripped over my own feet, so they made me be goalkeeper – and then I let all the goals in.

'Oh, he's so lovely!'

Gooner put his nose right up to her face, sniffed, and tried to lick her.

'Um, I wouldn't let him do that,' I said, quickly. 'He eats gross stuff.'

She laughed, digging in her pocket cos her phone was going off. She tugged it out and stared at it.

'I gotta go,' she said.

I stood up and got out of her way.

She slipped past me, rustling in her coat. The rain had stopped, and her coat was much too big for her, but she didn't unzip or take her hood down.

She started walking backwards, away from me.

'So what's YOUR name?' she said as she went.

'Me? Um, Wo—' I stopped and pretended to cough. Oh, I hated having such a weird name. People always gave me a funny look when I told them it.

'William,' I said. I coughed again.

Really? Was THAT a good idea? I rubbed my face and looked at the floor, confused by myself.

'Okay, William. Hey – you won't tell anyone that I was crying in a baby house, will you?'

I shook my head. Me? As if I'd ever tease anyone for crying. I was like *Prime Minister* of Crying. And I had no idea who this girl was or what she looked like under her coat.

'I don't know your name, anyway!' I said, shrugging.

'I . . .' she began, walking backwards again, slowly.

'OH! Stop!' I cried.

A worm . . . right by her foot. About to get squashed!

Before I could stop myself, I'd leapt forward and hooked the worm up with my finger, making her squeal and have to hop out of my way. 'Sorry! So sorry!' I spluttered, waving my closed fist at her. 'Worm.'

As if explaining helped.

Shut UP, Woody. Just don't talk.

'Worm?' she said. Her eyes crinkled, like she was giggling inside her hood. Laughing at me.

'Er . . yeah.' I shrugged. 'You were . . . cr . . . going to stand on it.'

I could feel the worm squirming in my hand – but not squirming as much as me.

'Oh, yeah, okay! Well, bye, William . . . gotta run!' she said. And with a wave, she broke into a sprint.

I watched her go.

Running away from weirdy me as fast as she could. Yep, I'd run away from me after that.

And for a minute there, I thought she might've actually LIKED me. I'd kept my weirdness in, and I'd nearly almost made a new friend.

Then I'd blown it.

And WHY did I say my name was William? What if I saw that girl again and she found out everyone really called me Woody? She'd think I was proper odd.

It was all round good work.

Un-weirding rules –
Don't try and be a worm hero and push girls over.

Also:

Don't randomly lie to people about your name.

You big TWERP!

Chapter 7

I felt awful on my way home.

Like there was no hope for me.

Gooner was better at making friends and being un-weird than I was.

I whipped in our back gate.

I was grumpy, and STARVING. As usual. Mum said I ate enough for four. But even though I couldn't wait to get my face in the bread bin, I still stopped to do what I always did· when I got back.

My new *strange* little habit: pretending to demolish my new school. I'd told myself if I didn't do it *every* time I came through the gate, then school would be TERRIBLE – even worse than I thought it was going to be. So now I HAD to do it.

Yeah, I know that was weird too . . .

I checked Mum wasn't around, and clambered on to the tree stump between the compost bin and the old hobbity-hut thing Shaun was building. He said it was going to be a wood-fired pizza oven, but so far it just looked like a dumb pile of mud.

I could just see the roof of the school in the gap between the houses, a few streets away. Just the sight of it made my belly go into a rock.

So I grabbed Shaun's spade handle like it was the rack-bar on my blasting machine, and dug it hard into the ground – BOOOOOOM! I fell on the lawn, rolling away commando-style like I'd been knocked down by the blast. I was imagining the school crumpling in a cloud of dust, like those YouTube clips of tumbling chimneys.

Ha, fall down, vile school. Right now.

Ah no . . . now I'd set Lu's dogs off with their

yapping. They were only as big as guinea pigs, but always on full-max volume.

Britney and Spears . . . a right couple of little numpties, they were. They always barked like it was *their* world, and everyone needed to get off it.

Lu lived over the fence at the bottom of our garden – and they were throwing themselves against it in a frenzy. It sounded like they were going to break right through the loose fence panel. It was only held up by two hooks, cos me and Lu used it to get into each other's garden without having to walk round the street way. When we were little we called it our secret tunnel. We'd draped it with sheets and pretended it was like a magic portal to Unicorn Land, or the sweet shop. Those were Lu's ideas. She'd always had better ideas for games than me – I just did what she said when I was little. Well, I still did actually, but I liked to keep that a bit quiet.

Yip yip yip YIP . . .

Gooner sighed like the noise was doing his

head in, and waddled towards the house. He was NOT mates with Britney and Spears – they made him look like an angel dog.

'Brit, Spears – get your bums in here NOW!' yelled Lu's mum.

In a few seconds, the barking stopped, and their back door slammed hard. The dogs always listened to her. But then I would too – Lu's mum was scary.

Peace at last . . . I jumped to my feet and had one more little go at demolishing the school.

BOOOOOOOM! Ahhhhh, it felt so gooooood!

Then I turned to follow Gooner indoors. And stopped mid-step. Because there was Shaun on the doorstep with a huge bowl of apple peelings.

He must've seen me BOOMing the school.

He grinned at me through his beard as he came across the lawn, walking in his funny way as usual. He always wore these silly flip-flops with thick socks. But he couldn't even walk properly in them and made a funny *shiffle-shuffle* as he went along, so Lu had started calling him Shuffly Shaun.

'So did it go down good?' he said, and made an exploding noise too. A pretty sharp one too – like he'd done it before.

I looked at him, surprised. Shaun was so soft. I didn't think he'd agree with pretend-demolishing things. I know Mum would've said it was being violent – even though I was OBVIOUSLY only messing around.

But I didn't let on to Shaun that I liked his noise. I just shrugged and walked past him.

I mean, Shaun was *all right* and everything – he was just annoying. A total hippy like Mum – except she was loud, bossy and busy, and Shaun just shuffled about quietly, humming and eating courgettes. The biggest problem was that, ever since he moved in with us two months ago, Mum'd been not-very-secretly trying to make him into my new dad. But just cos she was all lovey-dovey over him didn't mean I had to like him, did it?

No.

So I didn't.

And anyway I didn't need a new dad.

Especially not now . . .

I kicked my shoes off by the back door.

Gooner followed me in and went to the hall to flump in his smelly old bed.

The whole place stunk of vinegar – so strong that it stung the inside of my nose. Mum was sitting at the kitchen table, with a massive purple scarf thing tied round her head, making apple chutney.

'Hey,' she said, slicing a bad bit out of an apple, as I headed for the toaster. 'So how was the *visit*?'

'Um . . .'

What could I say that wouldn't make her cross?

Nothing about the photos. Or the cookies. *Or* the shopping trip. Or visiting the grave on the way back. And I definitely couldn't say that I thought Nan was nice, cos that'd get her way too moody.

'We had apple juice,' I muttered.

Mum stopped chopping and looked at me.

'Ye-e-e-s, but what did Barbie say? What does she want?'

'Er . . .' I started sawing off a hunk of bread from the loaf. 'Erm . . .'

Shaun came in just then and put the empty compost bowl on the table.

'She . . . er . . . just wants to get to know me, I s'pose,' I said. I stuffed a huge lump of bread in my mouth.

Shaun nodded like he thought that was cool, but Mum wrinkled her nose, making her nose-ring twitch, and did a huffing noise. She chopped an apple really hard, and began to say something, which I could tell wasn't going to be a kind thing. But then she glanced at Shaun and closed her mouth again.

It was so obvious that she just didn't want to be mean in front of Shaun. She was always trying to pretend to him that she was nicer than she really was. It really got on my nerves. Like, A LOT.

Except right now, it was handy.

I buttered another slab of bread at top speed. No time for toast – I was out of there.

I made for the kitchen door.

'Oh, Woods,' called Mum at my back. 'I found you a rucksack in the attic which'll do for school. It's nice and roomy, and it'll save us buying another one.' She pointed with her knife. 'It's on the chair there.'

I turned and looked at the bag on the chair in the corner, and groaned inside.

It was that colour Mum called 'orangey' but other people called pink, and the zip-pull was shaped like a heart.

'But Mum, isn't it a girl's bag?' I began through my cheekful of bread. Even though I knew there was no point.

Mum stopped mid-chop. 'Of course not, Woody. It's unisex,' she said, shaking her head like I was stupid.

Unisex? That meant for boys *and* girls, didn't it? Huh, only adults thought stuff like that – no kid alive would agree. My un-weirding-Woody plan would be totally ruined if I took *that* thing to school.

But there was just no arguing with Mum. I'd tried it with the school shoes she bought me and she hadn't listened at all. She said I was always growing out of my shoes, and now I fitted men's sizes, I was costing her a fortune. So she'd found me some cheap ones at the factory shop. But even though I was clueless about clothes, I could see they were old-man shoes.

So I just stayed quiet, took the rucksack and climbed the stairs. I threw the junky thing down, and sat on my bed. I could just never stick up for myself with Mum! And I had no one on my side. Shaun was too wet to pipe up, even if he didn't agree with her. Which he probably did anyway.

I got out my new phone and turned it over and over in my hands.

How could I get un-weird if Mum was dead set on dressing me like a cross between a girl and her granddad?

I chewed my lip.

All I wanted was some *normal* clothes.

And it looked like my only hope was to go on that shopping trip with Nan in the morning – even if I had to sneak out past Mum.

I took a big breath and joggled my phone in my hand. I had to do it – text Nan NOW.

I tugged the pink Post-it note out of my pocket, and stared at Nan's number.

Face the mall, Woody. Come on . . .

Hello. I can come shopping tomorrow. Thank you. From Woody.

I took me ages to write it, and my phone kept beeping cos I wasn't used to texting and my fingers were fumbly. Then I remembered just in time and changed it to *From William.*

SEND. There. No turning back now.

Nan replied immediately.

William, darling! That's marv. Pick you up at the bus-stop at ten. Babs x

William, William . . .

It must be such an easy name to have, cos it was so common. No one would ask you to repeat it like they did with Woody. That girl in the park hadn't blinked an eye when I'd said it.

I wished Mum had let me be William.

Like Dad . . .

I flopped back on my pillows.

A crazy thought had started wriggling in my brain:

What if I actually DID use the name William from now on? At my new school?

Could I?

I'd already be on the registers as William Woody Trindle. At primary school, supply teachers always called me William until I corrected them. But at Hawthorn I could just let the teachers carry on calling me it. Mum didn't even have to know.

A new, normal name . . . as part of my un-weirding plan.

I gulped.

Could I really pull it off?

Would I even remember? Forgetting your own name was weirder than having a strange one.

There was so much to think about.

I dug in my drawer for my notepad – the one I'd got for Christmas, which was made of recycled elephant poo. We couldn't have normal notepads in our house, could we? I wrote:

UN-WEIRDING RULES:
Be called William now.
Don't listen to Mum about anything to do with your life, ever.
Pretend you don't even know Mum outside of the house.

I read them through again, and thought they were definitely very reasonable. But then I tore out the page and screwed it up.

If Mum found my notebook, she'd make me into tofu fritters and fry me in organic garlic.

Chapter 8

'Woods!' Mum was yelling. 'Get the door, will you? We're busy.'

The doorbell went for the second time as I stomped downstairs.

Oh yes, they were so 'busy' . . .

Busy being embarrassing.

Shaun was sitting on the floor, strumming his guitar and humming a soppy song. Mum was sitting behind him on the sofa, massaging his neck and kissing the top of his head. I pulled the door shut so I didn't have to look.

For years, we'd called that room 'the Snug'

cos it was so small and cosy. But now that Mum and Shaun were always in there, all over each other, me and Lu'd renamed it 'the *Snog*'.

Jus*t bleugh*.

Gooner was in there too, asleep by the wood burner, playing gooseberry. I hoped those chips'd given him the farts . . .

I tugged open the front door.

'BOO!'

Lu bounced in at me with her little brother, Kai, in her arms. I never knew how she lugged him about: he was only two but *huge*, and she was so tiny and spindly. But then that was Lu all over – small but tough.

'BOO, BOO, BOOOOOOOOOOO!' Kai yelled, dropping his Scrumble Bear, and wriggling down out of Lu's arms.

'Sorry, we had to nip out the front way to dodge Mum,' said Lu, rolling her eyes. 'She's in a right stinking mood, so we've come to hide here for a bit. I thought we could have another quick round of Animal Snap? Get you some practice – you know, cos you're so rubbish.'

It was one of the silly games me and Lu had got into playing this summer. You had to make the animal noise instead of saying snap. It sounds babyish, but it was strangely hard and we just ended up in hysterics at the wrong noises we made. And that was the great thing about Lu. She'd known me so long, I could just be weird around her, and it was okay.

I nodded, grinning.

But then Kai flung himself at me.

'WOODY! Play wiv meeeeeeee!' he cried. I scooped him up and he put his nose against mine. He had a shiny, buttery face and smelt of Marmite toast, which was his favourite thing to eat.

Me and Kai were proper mates.

'Wotcha, Kaiser Chief!' I blew out my cheeks and did my Mr Potato-Head face. He roared with laughter and squidged my face with his little hands, puffing the air out.

'Story Sheeppppsssssss?' he cried, bouncing in my arms.

Story Sheeps was Kai's best game to play with

me – ever since he saw Mum's Story Sheep show at his friend Kaitlin's birthday party. I'd been there as Mum's helper – the Story Lamb, of course. The most enormous, clumsy lamb you ever saw.

I know. My weird, weird life . . .

But sometimes Mum *forced* me to help out at her extra-big parties. And I didn't mind it so much once I was there. I just spent most of my time crawling about baaaa-ing with little kids riding on my back. The worst part was the drive to the parties in the Story Sheep van, dressed in a lamb costume – I always ducked down in my seat in case someone saw me.

Un-weirding rule – Don't leave the house dressed as a giant baby animal.

I had loads of small fans though. At Kaitlin's party, Kai kept pushing all the other two-year-olds off me, screaming that I was KAI'S Story Sheeps and not theirs. And now whenever he saw me, he wanted a ride.

'Okay, buster – you got me!' I got down on all fours and Kai climbed on my back, while Lu plonked herself down on the bottom stair, grinning.

'BRA, BRA *back sheep* . . .' Kai sing-shouted, rocking and kicking me in the sides.

Yep, bra, bra . . . He just wouldn't have it that it was wrong.

'Hav oo any wools?

Nesir, nesir,

Free bags full!'

I did my job of being a very naughty Story Sheeps, turning and bucking until he slid off into a giggly pile.

Lu was sitting watching us, scratching at her arm – it looked like her eczema had flared up again. She'd had it for years, and of course Della had caught on to that, and nicknamed her Fleas. Not that Lu cared. She didn't get upset about stuff like I did.

'Hey, Woods!' she whispered, nudging me with her foot.

'Whug?' Kai was pulling my head round and

squashing my cheeks so my words were coming out wrong.

She pointed at the closed door of the Snog and mouthed, *'Are they in there?'* She made a kissy-kissy noise, and jabbed her finger in her mouth, pretending to be sick.

'Yeah,' I said.

'Look what I've found!' She did her panto-mime baddie snigger and waved a phone at me. 'It was right here on your hall table.'

Shaun's work phone! He hated mobiles as much as Mum did, but he had to have one for his veg-box delivery man job.

Uh-oh. This could lead to lots of trouble.

FOR ME.

Lu was poking at the phone, concentrating hard.

'Er . . . what you doing to it?' I asked with an *OOF* as Kai threw himself on to my back again.

'Pranking it, of course!' She giggled, her dark eyes glittering under her fringe. 'It's my duty.'

'Not again!' I said.

She'd pranked Shaun's phone about two

weeks ago. Somehow she programmed it so when he typed the words 'veg box', they changed automatically to 'BIG SMELLY PANTS'. So without realising it, he was texting all his customers stuff like: *'Hi, your BIG SMELLY PANTS bill is £14.'*

We nearly wet ourselves thinking about it – even though I was a bit worried he'd get the sack. But he didn't. And he didn't even tell Mum on us, even though he must've known we'd done it.

Lu tutted when I told her that.

'He's so WET!' she'd said. 'He can't even tell kids off.'

I carried on story-sheeping, but I had one eye on Lu.

Her and her pranks – she'd pranked me *loads* of times too. The last one was the fake dog poo on my bed, which I really thought Brits and Spears had done. Ha, ha, ha. But right now Shaun was Lu's main prank victim – ever since the day he moved in with us and I cried about it to her. She said she was on a mission to make him move out again.

I mean, I didn't mind – it was really funny, and I DID want Shaun to go away and stay there. But sometimes I had to stop her to save my own life. Like the time when she wanted to put cling film over the loo so Shaun would wee on the floor. Mum'd have done her nut.

The phone beeped and she tutted at it under her breath.

I chewed my lip, tipping Kai over my shoulder while he shrieked.

'Don't bust it, will you,' I said.

She waved me away. '*This*'ll make him shuffle away crying, for sure.' She held the phone in the air. 'There – I'm DONE!'

'What did you do to it?'

'You'll see,' she said, tapping the side of her nose, and grinning cheekily.

'You're so bad, Lu!' I said, smiling.

She did a curtsey. 'Thank you, fans, thank you!'

Chapter 9

Lu's own phone went off then. A text.

'Oh no, we gotta go. Mum's on at me,' she said, standing up and sighing. 'I have to help her with the washing. I'll beat you at Animal Snap next time. Come on, Kai.'

Kai fell to his knees.

'No, WOODY! PLAYYYYYYYYYYYYYY,' he wailed, tears brimming in his eyes. He stamped his foot and pulled his T-shirt up over his face, so just his baby pop-belly was showing.

'Kai! ' snapped Lu. She got annoyed when he nagged me all the time. But I could never say no to him. He had me round his chubby little finger.

'I know!' I said. I got down on all fours and crawled to the front door, opening it. 'Queue here for a Story Sheep ride to the front gate.'

Lu grinned at me gratefully.

Kai laughed, did this skippy dance and bounced on me.

'Wait, Kai!' said Lu. 'Your shoe's come off.'

Lu wrestled him on to her knee while he squealed.

So the sheeps had to wait on all fours, with his head half out the door. Gooner tugged the Snog door open a bit with his paw and came and stood in the doorway too – sniffing the street air and wagging his tail like he was so pleased I'd come to Goonerland on the floor.

But then a girl came along on the other side of the road.

Oh no!

I pulled Gooner back and shut the door quickly. No way was I getting caught by any girls being a Story Lamb.

I jumped up and peered round the hall curtain. It was Kendall. She used to be in my class at primary school, until two years ago when she'd moved to a different school. She was okay – kind of quiet.

But hang on . . . I moved to get a better look. What'd actually *happened* to her? She was wearing the kind of clothes older kids wore. She looked like a mini teenager now – like, she'd REALLY changed since I last saw her.

'Who you shutting out?' Lu said, still trying to help Kai with his shoe. Lu never missed anything. She had these X-ray eyes that noticed every small thing and looked right into your brain.

'Only Kendall. But hey, have you seen her recently?!' I said to Lu. 'She looks so different.'

'Yeah, I saw her the other day too,' said Lu in a bored voice. Kai had given up, and was lying on his back letting her do the Velcro on his shoe. 'Apparently she's gone boy-mad these days.' She brushed her hand through the air and did a pretend yawn. 'She's just SO mega annoying.'

Lots of people annoyed Lu. But lucky for me, if she liked you, she was super-loyal and the best friend ever.

At last Kai was ready. I pulled the door open and peered out. The coast was clear.

I gave him a bumpy sheep ride to the gate while he dug his sharp nails into my neck. I rolled him onto the lawn and staggered up.

'So see you tomorrow? Lu said, tugging the gate open.

'Um, I'm going shopping with my nan, actually,' I said.

'You? *Shopping?* Oh yeah, so how was it with your nan?

'Oh, all right. She's pretty nice, and she wants to take me to the mall, so . . .' I tailed off. I usually told Lu everything, but I suddenly didn't want to tell her about my un-weirding plan. I didn't think she would get it AT ALL.

'Okay, well, buy us a pressie!' she said. Kai was doing his funny toddler stumble along the street, so she ran to catch up with him, waving.

I closed the front door . . . and some loud music started blaring out.

It was Shaun's phone going off!

Full blast.

A tinkly, kiddie tune.

'I'm a little ballerina girl. Watch me leap. Watch me twirl . . .'

LUUUUUU!

I sniggered to myself, and legged it into the downstairs loo, out the way. I didn't know how Lu thought these things up.

I heard Shaun shuffle out.

I held my hand over my mouth.

The music went on and on.

I knew he was trying to work out what button to press – but he had no idea about his phone.

Finally the music stopped.

'What happened?!' called Mum from the Snog.

'Oh, it's just my phone playing up,' said Shaun.

No! Surely he knew we'd done it – it was so

obvious. Phones didn't just change their own ringtones or set their own alarms.

Why didn't Shaun ever dob us into Mum?

Lu *WAS* right: he couldn't stick up for himself – not with anyone.

Huh, and Mum was always telling ME that *I* needed to get braver. She joked that I was as nervy as one of those deer which dart away into the woods at the slightest leaf rustle.

But LOOK at her boyfriend!

Shaun was an actual grown-up, and he *w*as even *wimpier* than me.

He was like Mum's pet wuss.

I didn't know WHY he had to live in our house.

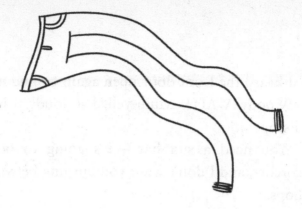

Chapter 10

'Yeah, Mum . . . Okay . . . yeah. I really have to go . . .'

She was still talking, but I closed the front door and belted down the path.

OMG, *Mum*!

I'd had to tell her about the shopping trip in the end – and cos Shaun wasn't there to make her nicer, she'd flipped her lid and gone on and ON for nearly half an hour about how we didn't need Nan's money and stuff. In the end, I'd just left early to get away from her.

No chance.

I heard the front door open again behind me.

'Woody, WAIT!' Mum yelled so loudly I had to stop.

'You need a sun hat – it's going to be a scorcher, and I don't want you burning between shops.'

WHAT?

I know I was pale and went pink at the slightest ray of sun, but wearing a sun hat in a *mall*? It was like Mum lay awake at night thinking up new ways to make me weird.

She was jogging towards me. Out in the street in her huge, bright green, onesie pyjamas and bobble slippers.

She stuffed a hat onto my head.

'There. It's Shaun's, but he won't mind.'

Shaun's hat. Oh, even better. His orange floppy cotton one with a plaited tassel. Just perfect for a mall.

But of course I'd do anything for a quiet life.

'Okay, thanks, Mum,' I said, tugging the hat onto my head. 'See you later.'

And pelted away from her with the hat-tassel

bouncing on my head like a little dumb ponytail.

As soon as I was at the bus stop, I took it off
and stuffed it into my pocket.

I sat on the bench to wait. I was so early.

I just hoped Della and Casey wouldn't come
past. And the sun was boiling me – probably
burning me too, like Mum said. I was too hot
in my clothes cos I'd chosen ones I thought Nan
might not hate – my T-shirt with a turtle on the
front, tucked into my best jogging bottoms, and
my blue Crocs. It probably wasn't a great look,
but it was my best shot.

A white Mini swept into the bus stop with a
toot.

Nan. And whoa – what an epic car!

I wasn't embarrassed to be seen in *that*.

She wound down the window and pushed her
sunglasses up on to her head, smiling. She had
painted her eyelids silver today.

'Hello sweetheart! Get in – let's go.'

The car smelt of new plastic and perfume.
She gave me a kiss as I strapped myself in, but

she missed again and got my ear with a big ziiiiing. It was still buzzing as she drove off.

Nan put some music on – just some normal stuff off the radio. Nothing like the whale-song music that Mum liked.

She kept smiling over at me all the way to the mall, like she was SO made up that I was there.

She pulled up in the mall car park.

'Right then, new clothes for my William!' she said, checking her make-up in the car mirror. 'It's going to be fun!'

I nodded, not feeling the fun-ness. There were loads of people in the car park – and other kids . . . My heart was racing as I got out of the car, but there was no going back now.

Nan took my arm firmly and led me in.

I'd never been in the mall before – Mum said it was tacky and over-priced.

But I thought it was all right – it had big, shiny floors, fountains and plants and stuff. A bit like the hotel in a James Bond film I watched at Lu's once.

Nan was wearing high heels and walked fast with a loud *click-click-click*, still clinging to my arm like she thought I might leg it. Which was completely possible.

We passed lots of shops – she seemed to know exactly where she was going – and then she stopped in front of a shop window.

'Here we are. This is where all the young people go, apparently,' she said, smiling like it was all such a big treat. 'I asked my neighbour Trudi, because she has teenagers.'

Uh? But I wasn't a teenager yet. And was it really a *shop*? It seriously looked more like a night-club disco sort of place. One you wouldn't get out of alive.

Its window had no clothes in it or anything – it was a just huge, black TV screen showing skateboarders doing flashy moves.

I followed Nan to the door and lurked in the doorway. Inside there were NO lights on at all – it was *completely* dark, and *boom-boom* music was blaring out.

Surely Nan wasn't serious?

'Come on – you're all right,' she said, grabbing my wrist. 'We'll ask someone to help us choose.' She pulled me into the darkness.

Okay, so there *were* actual clothes on hangers in there, and some tiny spotlights. But how could anyone see properly to buy stuff?

Nan hauled me over to one of the shop girls. I could only just see her face, but she looked like a model off the telly or something.

'Hi there!' she said smiling, flashing her white teeth in the gloom. She and Nan got chatting.

The girl had an American accent and a loud voice.

'So what size jeans do you wear?' she asked, turning to me.

'Er, size 10, I think,' I said, remembering the label in my old joggers.

'Um, that's women's sizing,' said the girl. She sounded like she was trying to hold in a giggle.

What?!

So it was true. Mum DID buy me ladies' clothes.

Just perfect.

'Never mind – I'll just pick out a bunch of sizes, and you can try things on,' she said, still sounding like she was laughing at me.

I was suddenly glad it was dark as my face was frazzling up.

I followed them around the shop as they moved along the rails, picking up armfuls of stuff. But I was banging into things and stepping on Nan's or the girl's toes. And Nan was calling me William, and I kept not realising she meant me, so I was sure the shop girl probably thought I was thick. In the end I gave up and just stood with my back against a pillar, staring at the shapes moving in the dark.

I'd had no idea that proper clothes shopping was like this – I'd only ever been to charity shops with Mum. I mean, wasn't *this* weird? No, it was probably just me, not understanding again.

They bundled me into a changing room – it was even dark in there too – and handed me piles of jeans and T-shirts and other things. I had to try them on, and then pull back the curtain for them to see how I looked.

All the clothes felt tight and I kept getting the jeans stuck over my big feet. But each time the girl said, 'Oh wow, yeah, he looks gre-a-a-t!'

I didn't know how she could tell – she must've had see-in-the-dark, carroty eyes.

It seemed to go on for hours, and I was starting to feel like I was being buried alive in a pit full of clothes and I'd never get out.

Nan brought me shoes to try on too. Dark-coloured shoes. And a jacket.

'Will . . . *Hello?* . . . William?'

Uh? Oh yes, that was me, wasn't it.

I pulled back the curtain.

'Right, I think we've got enough stuff now, darling,' smiled Nan. 'So why don't you just keep that last outfit on? You look so nice in it! We can take your old things in a bag.'

You mean, straight to the dump . . .

I bundled up my old clothes – I could hardly bend over, my jeans felt so skintight – and went and found Nan at the till. She'd bought me a rucksack too. A rucksack for school that wasn't for ladies. OH YES!

The girl packed everything into four huge bags. Nan must have spent every penny of her money.

'Thanks . . . er, thanks SO much,' I muttered. 'You got me tonnes.'

I'd only just met Nan and she'd already bought me more clothes than Mum'd ever bought me ever in my life – probably including my baby-gros.

'You're completely welcome,' Nan said. 'My pleasure.' And I knew she meant it.

We went out of the shop. It was so bright! I was blinking into the light.

'Ha, you look like you've just been born,' said Nan, laughing. 'But crikey – you do look *fab*. What a smartie!'

I caught my reflection in the TV-screen window, and at last I could clearly see what I was wearing.

Skinny black jeans like teenagers wear, a T-shirt with a surfer picture on it, and strange black shoes.

I was a completely different boy.

Chapter 11

'Haircut next?' Nan said. She was almost hopping – she was much more excited about all this than me.

'Um . . . okay,' I nodded, running my hand through my hair. Was my hair that terrible? It wasn't even in my eyes at the moment cos Mum had trimmed it the other day in the kitchen.

I trailed after Nan again through the crowds, feeling like an alien in my new stuff.

Nan led me into this smart hairdresser's, which was all white and smelt sweet – the same

whiff you get when you go past the girls'
changing rooms at school, sort of like Haribo
jellies.

Hair-dryers were blasting, music, and lots of
ladies dressed in black, talking.

'Not here for my highlights today, Kells.' Nan
smiled at one of the ladies by the till. 'We're
here to make my grandson even more handsome
than he already is.' Nan looked at me again like
she'd just won first prize, and I was it.

Then all the hairdresser ladies cooed at me
like I was a puppy or something.

'Oh, yes, isn't he a lovely boy! Good-looking
genes in your family, Babs!'

I lowered my head, blushing. I wanted one of
those invisibility cloaks. But instead I had a
teenager costume.

Then a pouty girl with stripy hair led me off
to have my hair washed, while Nan nattered on
to Kells.

I had to sit in a chair in front of a sink and
lie back so the girl could wash my hair backwards. She leant over me to turn the water on,

and I could see right up her nose, and her chest was sort of in my face.

I snapped my eyes shut quick so I didn't have to look. Oh no – this was all too much.

My face felt like it was literally frying. I knew I must've been the colour of ketchup.

Then when she sprayed the shower thing on my head, the water was too hot. It made me jolt a bit and I banged my head on the tap.

'Sorry love – you okay?' she said.

Was she trying not to laugh at me? Like that shop girl? Oh, what an idiot you are Woody! Winning all the prizes for awkward – as usual.

'Um, yeah, I'm fine,' I muttered, lying, and stopping myself from rubbing my throbbing head.

She started washing my hair with this bubbly shampoo that smelt like coconut Bounty bars.

'Do you want conditioner?' asked the girl, after she'd rinsed my head.

Conditioner? I'd never had that before. What was the right answer?

I shook my head and nodded at the same

time, and all the water went in my ears. 'Er, yes please?'

She smiled. Right answer. Phew.

But then she started talking to me about TV programmes Mum didn't let me watch, and I didn't know what to say. How do people do that chatting-to-strangers thing? I'd always been too shy. And now I was even more scared that I'd accidentally say something weird and break my un-weirding rules. So I stayed quiet and just said *mmm* a lot, and tried to nod in the right places.

I think I bored her, cos she stopped talking after a while. She wrapped my head in a towel, sat me in a seat to wait for the haircutting lady, and waved to a blond boy who was sitting waiting with his mum.

He came over for his hair-wash.

I hadn't seen him come in cos I'd had my head under a tap. He was about the same age as me, but was one of those cool, skateboarding kind of boys.

Hang on . . .

I swivelled round for a mo, pretended to look out the window, and glanced at his shoes and jeans.

Yes!

I had the SAME clothes on as him.

Nearly.

Un-weird clothes!

OH, THANK YOU, NAN. Being in that dark-disco shop had been worth it after all.

Kells came over with Nan and put a sort of bib on me.

Then Nan said quietly, as if my ears didn't work: 'His mother cut it with some old garden shears, by the looks. See if you can rescue it for him, poor kid.'

Kells started snipping and snipping. For *ages*. Mum usually only took about two minutes cutting round the edges. I felt silly looking at myself in the mirror, so I stared at the wall while Kells chattered on to Nan.

I could hear that blond boy having his hair washed behind me. The hair-wash girl was talking to him like she had to me. Except he was chatting back. I found out that he was called Josh, and was starting Hawthorn tomorrow too.

'Oh, same as William over there,' said the girl. Nan'd told everyone everything about me.

I looked in the mirror and Josh gave me a quick thumbs-up, as the girl towel-dried him. I tried to do it back, but I got my thumb caught up in my bib thing. I fumbled around trying to get my hand out, but Josh had lost interest by then – he'd already gone back to talking to the girl.

Un-weirding rule – Don't get tangled up in bibs like a Mr Magoo.

They were talking about this outside gym thing he did called parkour, which the hair-wash girl's boyfriend did too. I'd never heard of it, but it seemed to be about doing back-flips off benches, jumping over bins, and running over roofs. It sounded like extreme gym for super-cool people. Not something I could ever do without involving an ambulance.

Kells started hair-drying me so I couldn't eavesdrop Josh any more.

'There you go, precious – take a good look,' she said afterwards, putting some blue jelly stuff on my hair.

I looked at myself then. My eyes went wide in the mirror.

Blimey, I looked *really* different now. My hair was smooth and quiffed up at the front, and so short you could see all of my ears. It was a proper, normal haircut.

'Oh, so snazzy,' Nan said. 'My handsome William number 2.'

We stood by the till while Nan paid Kelly LOADS of money – so many tenners.

I caught a glimpse of myself in a long mirror. The whole of me – hair and clothes. Top to toe.

IT HAD WORKED!

I had *completely* un-weirded myself. On the outside at least.

Huzzah!

Then I saw the hair-wash girl appear with some squash and a chocolate Hobnob. She took them over to Josh, who was waiting for his haircut.

WHAT?

She hadn't got ME that!

My heart kind of sank again.

Josh had made best friends with the hair-wash girl in ten minutes flat. And all I'd managed to say was *um*.

I sighed. Un-weirding was a very good start. But clearly there was going to be *much* more to this making-new-friends thing than that.

HOW was I going to do it?

And school started in just twenty hours thirty-five minutes.

Chapter 12

Nan pulled up at the bus stop to drop me off.

'Thanks so much,' I mumbled. 'For everything!' I didn't know how to be more grateful without getting an actual THANK YOU NAN! T-shirt made.

Nan drove off with a happy toot, leaving me standing there, surrounded by bags, and crumpled up with shyness to be back near home in my new get-up.

I pulled up my hood and jogged home in a rustle of bags. I had to get off the streets, but I was NOT looking forward to facing Mum.

Gooner went loony when I opened the front door. But then he stood looking at me, like he couldn't work out what was different. Maybe my clothes smelt of shops.

'Stop staring at me, you wombat!' I said to him, ruffling his ears. Even Gooner was making me feel awkward.

Mum heard the door go, and came out of the kitchen in a waft of frying onions and garlic, drying her hands.

Wait for it . . .

'Oh. My. GOD!' she gasped, stopping and looking me up and down.

'What?' I said. I ran my hands over my hair. '*What?*' She was making me want to dive under the hall rug. Even worse than I'd expected.

'You . . . you . . . just look like a *teenager* . . . and so much like HIM! It's like you're *channelling* him!' said Mum.

Him clearly meant Dad. But what was she on about?

'*Channelling?*'

'It means . . . it's almost like he's living

95

through you,' she said, looking at me again and shaking her head.

Trust Mum to say weird hippy stuff like that. I bit my lip and tried to put my hands in my pockets, but my jeans were too tight.

'I know you've always been very much like him, but now with that hair . . . it's unreal.' Mum was still ogling me.

God, Mum – it's just a haircut. People look like their dads. Calm down.

Anyway, I WANTED to look like him, didn't I?

I tried to edge past her towards the stairs. But –

'And Barbie bought you ALL that too!' she spluttered, pointing at all the bags.

'Er . . . um . . . yeah,' I shrugged.

Shaun came out the kitchen and wolf-whistled at me.

'Looking fresh, Woods,' he said.

Mum's hands were on her hips, and she was glaring at my bags like they were full of dead rats. I knew she was holding in a hissy fit. But now Shaun was there, so she had to be all nicey-nice.

'Your nan got you some new stuff, then?' said Shaun, nodding at the bags. 'Brilliant.'

I nodded, and then shook my head at him. Was he that dim? Hadn't he noticed Mum's face? Did he want to die?

Even Mum was looking at him in surprise.

'Anyways, tea's up,' said Shaun, shuffling into the kitchen, just as the doorbell went.

'I'll get it!' I yelled too loudly and keenly, like I was four and doorbells were the most exciting thing ever. I threw myself at the front door.

Mum scowled off after Shaun into the kitchen. But I knew I hadn't heard the last of it from her – no such luck.

It was Lu.

'We need Scrumble Bear NOW. I think Kai left him here?' she said, breathlessly. 'It's an emergency. We might even need helicopters! He's having a meltdown with Mum at home, and she has to go to work and –' She stopped and looked me up and down, just like Mum had. 'What

ARE you wearing? And what's going on with your hair?'

'Um, yeah, I went shopping with my nan, remember. And to the hairdresser.' I felt my cheeks getting hot.

'Oh,' she said. Then she frowned: 'So . . . are you trying to be all fashionable now or something? Pretending you're in Year Ten?'

Ouch.

I scuffed my toe into a spot on the carpet. Why was everyone on my case?

'No . . . I . . . er . . .' I didn't know what to say.

I spotted Scrumble Bear's paw under the coats in the corner of the hall. I nabbed him and handed him to Lu.

Her eyes had softened. She knew she'd been a bit nasty.

'I meant, you look older,' she said. 'Anyway, got to go!' And she stuffed Scrumble Bear under her arm and marched down the path.

But she turned at the gate and called back to me, 'Yeah, so, Woods – good luck with big school tomorrow, yeah? I'm lucky, I've got an inset day!' I nodded, and made a shudder-face at the word *school*.

She put her head on one side, swinging the gate with her foot.

'Hey, I'll come and walk to school with you on your first day, if you like – I've got nothing to do in the morning.'

I knew this was her way of being sorry, without actually saying it.

I nodded gratefully.

'Thanks. Yeah, that'd be great.'

'Okay, I'll meet you on the corner then. At quarter to eight. I know how you like to be early!'

I gave her a big smile.

She did know.

She could be a bit harsh sometimes, but I could take it – she was my mate.

And I was so glad that she was walking with me in the morning.

Chapter 13

I went to bed early.

Not that I could sleep.

My mind was too full of school, and I felt like puking. Like I was on Death Row or something, and tomorrow was going to be the End Of Me.

I was trying to memorise my un-weirding rules, as if I was revising for a test. Because I was going to have to watch myself for weirdness *all the time.*

I kicked off my duvet.

Maybe I should even write the rules on my sleeve.

Or maybe NOT. See? There I went again.
Thinking up weird stuff.

Un-weirding rule - Don't write all over your
clothes = no one does that!

I rolled over and closed my eyes tight.

Having un-weird clothes and rules was great.
At least I wouldn't stick out like a sore thumb
now. Which might stop kids from laughing at
me, or worse, bullying me.

But I still felt sick with worry. That Josh boy
had made me realise un-weirding wouldn't be
enough to get me new mates. I was going to be
a loner forever.

I just had no idea how Josh had managed to
make friends with that hair-wash girl so fast.

He'd been . . . what? . . . not shy . . . all
chatty. And smiley and charming too.

My eyes flicked open.

Yes, that was it. Josh had charmed her.

He'd been a right little charmer.

Like Nan said Dad was!

Except Dad believed he got *his* charm from that golden Rubik's Cube. His make-you-charming charm.

Nan thought it was a load of superstitious rubbish, and it did seem *a bit* mad. But maybe not any madder than believing in auras and star signs and crystal healing, which were just *normal* in our house, and . . . WHAT IF IT REALLY WAS TRUE?

My heart began beating faster.

I sat up.

AND WHAT IF THE CHARM WOULD WORK FOR ME TOO?

I knew it was Dad's, and so it probably wouldn't. Like in Harry Potter, where wands wouldn't work properly for anyone but their owners. But who knew?

I could at least ask to *borrow* the cube, and SEE if it worked for me.

I needed as much charm as I could get tomorrow.

And what did I have to lose?

I'd ring Nan now.

I turned my lamp on and picked up my phone.

I started to press buttons for her number, but then I tossed my phone back on my bedside table and clicked the light off again.

I just couldn't ask her.

She kept the charm on an actual *velvet cushion* in a glass case, like it was treasure. And it was her dead son's *most precious* thing. She'd said that.

It'd be so rude to ask. She might be cross. Or even CRY.

And anyway the charm probably *did* only work for Dad.

I picked up my legs and flopped them out on top of my duvet with a sigh. I'd just have to manage. Keep my head down, be un-weird, and hope for the best.

But I didn't feel hopeful.

Because if starting secondary was a computer game, un-weirding only put me on about Level 3, and charmers like Josh would be on Level 4879865.

Bah.

I was going to be at the bottom of the pile.

And there was only ten hours sixteen minutes to go.

Chapter 14

I woke up and froze, as my brain switched on to the horrible, disgusting truth.

Today was the first day of term.

Butterflies caught in my throat, and this cold, jelly-like feeling spread through me.

I couldn't face it.

Except I had to. I was meeting Lu at quarter to eight.

I made myself get up, and forced on my uniform. My tie was wonky and strangling me. But at least my shoes, coat and bag would be the same as everyone else's – hopefully. NO thanks *at all* to Mum; big thanks to Nan.

I was just hiding the hideous shoes Mum had got me when a bird landed on my windowsill and made me jump.

A magpie.

What was that rhyme? *One for sorrow. Two for joy . . . ?*

I rushed to the window to look for a second one, cos I could use some joy today. But there was only one, all by itself on our shed roof.

Great. A birdy curse. That was all I needed.

Quick – touch wood!

I hugged my wooden wardrobe. Then I clumped down the stairs, touching everything wooden I could see. I'd better touch all the wood I could before I stepped out the door.

Un-weirding rule – Don't cuddle furniture at school.

Oh no – I was beyond help. Shaun and Mum were sitting at the kitchen table in their dressing gowns, munching matching bowls of home-made muesli and soya milk.

'Hey, Woods. Up bright and early, ready for your first day, eh?' said Mum, through a noisy mouthful.

'Hmmm,' I muttered, stuffing some bread into the toaster. Yeah, great, Mum. I can't wait.

I wasn't hungry at all, but I didn't want my tummy to rumble in first lesson. Everyone would turn and stare at me.

'I remember my first day. It was such a lark . . .' began Mum.

Ugh, please stop! I didn't want to listen to one of her everything-is-awesome stories now. I flicked my toast out before it was done and tried to butter it, but it just ripped. So I gave up, folded it into my mouth and turned to scuttle out.

'Oh, I made your packed lunch, Woods,' said Mum, before I got to the door. 'It's on the side there.'

I mumbled thanks, grabbed the lunchbox and hurried out into the hall. I opened the box and

. . . poooooeeee! A super-garlicky, home-made hummus sarnie made with sprouted black bread, a hard-boiled egg and a raw carrot.

Great.

Everyone else'd probably have white-bread ham rolls and Hula Hoops, just like at primary school. *No one* else had odd hippy lunches like mine – no one. There was no way I was opening that weirdy stinkbox at my new school.

Un-weirding rule – Don't eat food that means people need gas masks to talk to you.

I shut the lid. Where could I hide it?

I spotted Gooner through the Snog door.

Aha, of course. I could hide the lunch inside Gooner.

He was lying on the sofa – which was VERY naughty and VERY illegal. He knew he wasn't supposed to, so he usually scrambled off when he heard someone coming, and got in his bed with an innocent face, trying to pretend he hadn't done it. But he was so completely asleep that he hadn't heard me.

I went over to him.

He was having one of his doggy dreams. His paws were twitching and he was whimpering and growling like he was fighting big, scary dream-dogs bravely in his sleep. In real life, he wouldn't fight a tiny Chihuahua, even if it was chewing his leg off – he'd just run away. He was a big wuss like me.

'Oi, wake up, you sofa criminal!' I said to him, joggling his chubby tummy with my foot.

Gooner jerked out of his dream and blinked at me with a tiny, sleepy wag. Then straight away his nose started going mad with fast sniffing. Yeah, even with the lid shut, the garlic pong was enough to wake the whole galaxy up.

'Want a special-treat breakfast, huffalump?'

Of course he did.

He staggered off the sofa, looking all bad-hair-day-ish. He shook himself, yawned and stretched his paws out in front with his bum in the air, wagging his tail at me.

I fed him the sandwich and the egg. He wolfed them down in two gulps, and then looked for more.

'All gone, Furball.' I ruffled his head. 'And I'm not taking you out this morning. Go and see Shaun today. Ooh, you got garlic breath!"

It was usually my job to take him for a walk round the block in the morning. But Shaun'd said he'd do it for the first week at my new school – probably just to get gold stars from Mum.

I hid the lunchbox behind the sofa, and ran back upstairs. I shook some pound coins out of my pocket money jar. I'd buy chips from the canteen. Mum'd never know . . .

I tiptoed back down.

Gooner'd got back on the sofa, but I didn't tell him off. I opened the front door extra quietly.

'Bye,' I called out at the last second.

Then I zoomed off down our path before Mum could catch me.

Chapter 15

I walked round the corner towards Lu's house – and towards school.

There was no one about yet – only a few adults in office clothes. The streets were so quiet, I could hear my new shoes squeaking as I walked . . . *very* slowly. Like my school was Mordor, and I was going to my doom.

I sat on the wall outside Lu's flat and waited. The air had a bit of a nip and smelt autumn-ish already.

I looked at my watch. Come on then, Lu! It wasn't like her to be late. And I was on danger-alert look-out for Della. I didn't know which bus stop she'd go to for her new school. But I did NOT want to see her for any fun early morning chats. Or Casey. It was going to be bad enough trying to dodge HER all day at school.

Another lone magpie bobbed into the tree opposite.

Oh, just bog off, birds.

I made sure no one was looking, and then I leant back and patted a tree trunk. And then my own wooden head too.

Finally there was a clatter and Lu's front door opened.

'Sorry, sorry – I'm coming!' She looked pink in the face. She lowered her voice. 'Mum is MAKING me bring Kai cos she says she's got to hoover. So I'm going to walk with you and then go to the park.'

She looked at me hard then. 'Blimey, you really do look so different,' she said. 'Like, you're NOT you.'

I didn't know what to say, so I just shrugged. I WANTED to look different if that meant un-weird and like Dad. But Lu was making me feel uncomfortable – giving me one of her suspicious looks like she thought I was up to something dodgy.

She went back into her hall and backed out with the pushchair. Kai was nattering to himself, and stuffing his face from a lunchbox FULL of small Marmite sandwiches. It looked like he had about forty of them.

Then Lu nipped back in again for Britney and Spears, who immediately went mental with barking. Oh no, did *they* have to come too? I hadn't expected THIS! I'd wanted to walk quietly to school with Lu. Not in some kind of noisy, Marmite-y, weirdo carnival that everyone would stare at.

But I had no choice.

We walked along in a massive cloud of bark.

School wasn't far and we got to the gates in no time.

It was only five to eight.

We were so early. *Ridiculously* early. The school looked all closed up.

What now? I had this thing about not being late, but being this early was dumb. And probably weird.

I paced up and down, my tummy feeling quivery while Lu fought with the pushchair brake.

At least the dogs were quiet. They were pulling on their leads to sniff around the bottom of a lamp-post, wagging their tails.

'We'll just wait with you. We could just sit on that wall there,' said Lu, pointing. 'Now these two have shut their gobs.'

But she spoke WAAAY too soon.

Some Hawthorn boys about my age came round the corner, kicking a ball, and set them off yapping again.

The boys all turned to look over at us. I felt my face begin to burn up. I just wanted to blend in – be normal. But with this lot with me, I felt like I had a flashing siren on my head.

Kai finished his sandwich mountain and threw his box on the ground, arching his back in his pushchair, instantly bored.

'OUT!' he yelled. 'Kai out now!'

'Okay, in a minute,' said Lu, yanking at the dogs, who were making my ears burst. Then Britney managed to twist her lead right round both our legs, tying me and Lu together. Lu held on to me and untangled us, giggling.

Out the corner of my eye, I could see the boys looking over, nudging each other and smirking.

Laughing at the weirdy circus show that was us.

'OUTTTTT, Woodeeeee!' Kai screeched, reaching for my hand.

Any minute now, he was going to start asking for Story Sheeps or Mr Potato Head. In the street.

This was NOT supposed to happen!

Not today.

I felt hot and dizzy.

I was going under.

'Er, listen,' I stammered to Lu. 'I'd better go in. It's probably time. You should go to the park now.'

'What?' she said. 'But there's no one there yet, Woody – look.'

'Um, I think I saw someone unlock the door. Like a teacher,' I mumbled, feeling a whoosh of heat at my humongous lying.

My really *bad* lying.

Lu glared at the ground, scratching her arm hard over her sleeve.

'Oh, right, I get it,' she snapped.

'What? No, I –'

'You've got too cool to be seen with us now, yeah?!' She glowered at me from under her dark fringe, her eyes all frosty.

I felt panic bubbling up in me.

'No, it's not YOU, Lu . . . it's just . . . um . . .'

'So it's Kai, is it? He can't help it – he's only two!'

I opened my mouth again, but she put her hand up to cut me off, lasering me with her eyes. Then she turned and stalked off, pushing Kai, who was screaming his nut off for me, and dragging the dogs in a knot of leads behind.

My shoulders sagged as I watched her go, and tears blurred my eyes.

I was so glad I didn't have to wait with them.

But now I'd done it.

She thought I was embarrassed by them.

Which I was.

How nasty was that? They were my best friends . . . and now I was CRYING by the school gates.

Un-weirding rule *very important* – DO NOT BLUB AT SCHOOL, WOODY! Just don't.

But I couldn't stop. I was breaking that no-tears rule before registration. IN FRONT OF SOME NEW KIDS.

I made a bit of a show of walking into school in case Lu turned round, and then nipped in behind the school hedge.

And there I was. Hiding in a bush again, sniffling. Weirdy, wussy Woody had struck again.

I was staying here too. I just couldn't face today now. I looked at the school building through the leaves, and my guts turned over, and even more tears came. My un-weirding rules

DEFINITELY weren't enough to get me quietly through today – not even nearly.

School was cancelled.

I did a sigh which came out like an odd gulpy sob.

I bet my dad never hid from school in a bush.

Chapter 16

It took me a while to get brave enough, but eventually I got out Nan's old phone and dialled her number from the bush.

'Nan – it's Wood—. Er . . . William. Er, look, would you mind . . . I mean . . . do you think I could . . . er . . . like *borrow* Dad's Rubik's Cube-charm, please? Just for today?'

I still didn't want to ask her – but now things had got DESPERATE. It really felt like my ONLY way out of this hedge.

'I promise to look after it!' I said in a small voice, wincing.

I held my breath and crossed my fingers.

'*Really?!* Oh, thanks so much!' I breathed. 'Okay, I'll meet you on the corner. You know – by the park.'

By the graveyard . . .

Amazing! She was bringing it to me – and she didn't sound like she minded at all. I VOTE NAN!

I sidled out of the bush, peering around. Lu had gone, but the boys were all still there.

I hurried through the middle of them, with my hood up in case my eyes were red, and ran along the road.

Nan was there before me in her car, the engine still running. She wound down her window.

'Oh, look at you in your Hawthorn uniform,' she sighed. 'It's hardly changed at all. Takes me back.' Then she handed me the cube, blowing a kiss.

'There you go then – one charm!' she said, beaming. 'I don't know, you boys! You're just so much like him, aren't you! Have a lovely day, babe.'

'Thank you!' I waved her off, with the cube tight in my fist.

I had it.

I actually HAD it!

I waited, still waving, until Nan turned the corner. Then I crossed over and flew through the graveyard gate. Ten past eight. I just had time if I got a move on. And this was the important bit . . .

I had the charm – but it felt like I needed Dad to *activate* it. After all, it was HIS. And I needed his permission.

Even if that was mad.

I slowed to a walk and went over to Dad's grave.

I put my hand on the cold stone.

'I've got your charm now – hope that's okay. Thanks so much for lending.' My voice had gone all odd and croaky. 'I know it's yours, but please could you make it work on *me* too? I need to be like you, see. *Exactly* as charming as you.'

I paused, and then added in a whisper:

'I need your help today, Dad.'

Chapter 17

DONG!

The church bells were ringing for quarter past eight. I had to head to school now or I'd be late.

I said goodbye to Dad, and ducked out of the graveyard, polishing the cube on my sleeve, so it shone gold in the light.

It really did feel like treasure. Like a precious, special thing.

BUT WOULD IT WORK ON ME?

I hoped Dad *would* let it work on me too, if he could. I was his son, after all.

The thing was – how would I even know if it *was* working?

What I needed was a TEST. Someone to try it out on.

If I dared . . .

And just as I thought that, I turned a corner and there was Kendall, in her Hawthorn uniform, up ahead of me, her curly ponytail bobbing. I slowed down. Maybe she'd do as my guinea pig? She wouldn't be TOO scary to try the charm out on.

My heart did a blip as I did longer steps to catch her up.

What if I tested it on her and she just said *push off Weirdy Woody* and walked away? That'd be HORRENDOUS. And I'd have to see her at school in a minute.

I was right behind her now.

I had to stop dithering and just do it. I had to find out if it would work. It was now or never.

I moved alongside her.

I could see her jaws going, chewing her gum.

I knew she must've seen me, but she was ignoring me completely, as usual.

I pressed the charm into my hand so hard it hurt.

Make me into a charmer-boy, please!

I took a deep breath and imagined the charm's power zinging into me, just like it had with Dad.

I put my head up, feeling braver.

'Hi, Kendall!' I said, smiling. I looked her right in the eye so I could see if the charm was working.

She sort of jumped. 'Oh hi . . . er? . . . Woody!' she said, with a big grin. 'You all right?'

I nodded and walked on, overtaking her.

Okay, so she'd said hi. And she'd grinned. That was good, wasn't it? She'd never *ever* speak to me normally, so it must've been the charm that made her do it.

Surely?

Well, *maybe* . . .

I sighed, rolling the cube in my hand.

It hadn't really been the greatest test.

But before I'd even taken many more steps I heard stampy footsteps behind me and:

'Hey, Woody!'

I whirled around. It was Kendall again.

'Er . . . hi,' I said. I slid the charm into my pocket out of sight.

'Um . . . is it okay if I walk with you?' she asked, blushing. 'You know, to school?

Really?

'Yep, okay,' I said. Then I had no idea what to say to her. We walked along in silence, and I stared at the road like cars were very interesting, feeling my face blushing up. Kendall was chewing on her gum, and giving me little glances and smiles.

She had this shiny stuff on her lips. Was she wearing *lipstick*? For school?

'I like your new haircut,' she said.

Then she went pink too. She was being so strange. Friendly. I wasn't used to it. Did she like me cos I was un-weirded? Surely she wouldn't be suddenly THIS nice – not just cos of my new hair.

I squinted my eyes and nipped a sly look at her. She noticed and gave me a huge smile.

No, it had to be the charm.

Oh. My. God.

It looked like it WAS actually working for me. Maybe Dad really had *activated* it for me.

And it was making Kendall stick to me like Velcro – if I slowed down so did she. Talking-talking-talking in a fast, gushy way about random stuff.

'Oh, and I *really* love your new bag, Woody!' she said, breathlessly. 'It's lush.'

I remembered to smile at her – as charming as I could – like Dad was doing in all those photos. Then I thought maybe I was over-doing it – smiling like a toothy Wallace and Gromit cartoon. Yes, I definitely needed to tone it down a bit.

But then I had this thought.

Could I test the name William out on her too? Like a rehearsal. Seeing as she seemed to be, well, so *charmed*.

Kendall was talking again, but I did a sort of

cough thing, and picked a leaf off a hedge and ripped it up. Trying to be casual, but I think it just turned out weird.

'Actually I'm called William now,' I muttered, interrupting her. 'William is my real first name, see, not Woody.'

I glanced over at Kendall as we walked, to try and catch her reaction.

She nodded hard and flicked her ponytail behind her, wafting some girly-ish perfume, like a flowers smell.

'Oh, okay! Yeah, yeah, that suits you! It's cute,' she said, beaming.

Well, that was easy.

I could feel a grin spreading over my face. And then I stopped it.

Un-weirding rule – Don't randomly grin to yourself.

So I just grinned a lot on the inside.

THE CHARM WAS WORKING FOR ME TOO!

I'd asked for Dad's help – and he'd made it happen. It honestly did seem like that. I'd wanted it to be true so much, and now it was starting to FEEL true.

And just in time for my first day at school too. Like being rescued by Batman from the evil baddies at the very last minute.

I felt a lump rise up in my throat then and I gulped it down.

Or rescued by my own dad.

Chapter 18

We followed the flow of kids along the road. As we turned into the school gates, I came over all shaky again.

There were swarms of kids *everywhere*. Huge ones from older years, and then small Year Sevens wearing brand new uniforms and rucksacks so big they could've lived inside them like tent-homes. All of them shouting and calling to each other. The noise made my ears whirr as I pushed through into the school entrance and down a corridor. I was stooping so I didn't feel so tall and sticking-up-above, and my insides were rolling over and over.

I got out my charm again.

Kendall got bounced on by some friends in the crowd, so I was left by myself.

I unfolded my school map and stared at it.

I had to find Block D, room 17 – my tutor room.

We'd all been shown the way there at the Induction Day, and it'd seemed easy-peasy then. But now my brain was mush; my map could've been of Portugal for all the use it was. I was sure the school must have grown over the holidays.

I was clinging to the cube so hard its corners were making dents in my hand, and trying not to get in a state. But my charm wasn't going to help me find my way. It might make me more charming, but it wasn't a sat nav.

I'd tried following other Year Seven kids. Which was of course a stupid idea cos none of them were in my tutor group. Duh. And then when I passed a poster about eating healthy food for the second time, I knew I was definitely,

definitely going round in circles. My head was swimming, and the whole thing was reminding me of our school trip to a maze in Year One when I'd got lost and cried. I was THIS close to crying again now too. No, NO – remember that un-weirding rule!

In fact I still needed to remember ALL my un-weirding rules if I wasn't going to undo the charm's good work.

I bundled into a gap between some lockers, sniffed hard, and stared at the map, turning it this way and that, my heart galloping.

Try and breathe, and just *look*, you dimwit.

Block D was the orange one, so I *was* actually in the right building. And room 17 should be just up the corridor. I must've walked right past it. I stepped out into the stream of kids – and crashed straight back into my hidey-hole again.

Casey!

She came wandering past me, by herself, peering in classroom doors, and up and down the corridor, clearly with no idea what she was doing. She didn't even have a map.

Her shoulders were all hunched up and kids were knocking into her as they passed, but she wasn't saying anything. She looked so small and worried. I'd never ever seen HER look like that before.

For a tiny minute I even felt a bit sorry for her. But then I remembered that she was the same Casey who'd helped Della write my name in some school library books so I got in a tonne of trouble. The same Casey who'd laughed while Della put hay from the class hamster cage in my lunchbox.

Then I didn't feel so sorry for her any more.

DRRRRRRRRRRRRINGGGG!

A bell went right by my ear and made me jump. Secondary-school bells were so LOUD!

And that bell meant I was supposed to be at registration in my tutor room *right now*.

I waited a second longer to let Casey go wobbling off round the corner, then I picked my way down the corridor, through the crowds.

And there was room 17.

At flipping last.

Chapter 19

Our tutor, Mrs Jollans, gave me a kind smile as I went in and nodded at me to find a seat. Lots of kids were sitting at desks, waiting, fiddling with new-looking pencil cases.

As I walked across the room, their eyes on me felt like hot, zapping rays. I swung down into a desk in the middle row against the wall. Tucked away, less noticeable. If I could've painted myself pale green like the wall, I would've rollered my own face.

I glanced around. I recognised some of the kids from our Induction Day, but no one from my old primary. No one was talking much.

My stomach was in a ball. I was fiddling with the charm-cube, twisting it, and then re-doing it to pass the time. To calm myself.

I could see my broken-up reflection in its shiny sides.

Maybe Dad had looked at his face in it too . . .

Mrs Jollans started chatting to the boys at the front about their holiday. She seemed like a nice, funny teacher – much less scary than all the kids. In fact it'd be easier to hang out with *her* at breaktime.

Ha, great. Way to go, Woody. THAT would help your popularity.

Un-weirding rule – Don't be best friends with any teachers. Or any dinner ladies.

Two girls hurried through the door. The first one had yellow curly hair and a smiley face. She looked round the room, and grinned at me.

At *me*?

I looked behind, but she really *was* looking right at me. And making a beeline for the empty seat next to me. Did I know her?

'Hey!' she said, as she sat down. 'I'm Anna!'

'Oh, er . . . hi. I'm W—' But I stopped mid-word, my eyes boggling, my heart doing a huge blip.

The girl who'd come in with Anna was CASEY.

Casey was in my tutor group? No wayyyyyyy! But she hadn't been here on the Induction Day! This was *hideous!* She'd start a Weirdy-Woody Baiting Club in this tutor group. Which would meet EVERY MORNING.

I felt my ears burning hot.

Casey had followed Anna across the room, like she was sewn to her. She looked around desperately for a seat next to Anna, but there wasn't one. I was in it.

And then at last, she looked at me and did a huge double-take.

I braced myself . . .

But Anna smiled up at her, and then turned

to me and gave me an even bigger smile.

Casey watched Anna and frowned. Then she just stood there looking hopeless, like she wanted to sit on Anna's lap.

And I suddenly saw for the first time that without Della, she wasn't cocky at all. She was like a tail without a dog to wag her.

She was looking for a new person to cling on to – and she'd picked Anna.

But Anna seemed much more interested in being friends with *me*.

Oh YESSSSS! This was the charm doing its stuff again. It had to be. No one normally liked me – no one apart from Lu.

Mrs Jollans asked Casey to sit down, and began talking to the class. Casey sighed dramatically, slouched over to a desk in the middle of the room and flopped into the seat with a scowl. But she kept looking over – not to give me evils – but trying to catch Anna's eye. And sometimes Anna smiled at her, but then she was being friendly with everyone.

Including me. In fact, *especially* me.

I realised I was grinning to myself again, so I made my face stop.

'Esther Browning?' called Mrs Jollans.

The register! I felt my insides flip over.

'Corinne Harragin?'

'Louis Jackson?'

This was it . . . the moment when I *wouldn't* mumble my usual line when new teachers did the register – er-*actually-Miss-my-name's-Woody.* The moment my name would become un-weird William. Just like my dad.

Mrs Jollans was getting nearer my name.

'Eddie Saunders?'

'Beth Solman?'

But what if Casey jeered?

I looked across at her.

She was biro-ing tattoos on her own arm. Her long hair had fallen around her face, like a curtain she was trying to hide behind. Somehow she didn't look *at all* menacing any more, sat there like that. I had a feeling that she just wouldn't pipe up.

'William Trindle?'

Me.

But I just sat there with my mouth open like a Muppet, with my charm sweaty in my fist.

Anna nudged me in the ribs.

'That's you, isn't it? William?'

She broke my trance. I made a noise that sounded like a mix between a sneeze and *Yesh Mish*.

Then Anna grinned at me, Casey carried on biro-ing herself, and no one had said anything.

Yes!

I gave Anna a quick thumbs-up for saving me, although I actually had no idea how she knew my name.

Then I sat and smiled inside.

I'd done it . . .

Goodbye Woody.

Hello William.

Chapter 20

The morning was taking up all my energy and brainpower and bravery. I felt like I was being flung about on a fairground ride.

So many people to deal with . . .

So many *charmed* people.

Like a boy called Alfie who sat next to me in French and told me bad jokes all lesson. And the two girls in the corridor who told me they liked my bag. I mean, it was all good – *amazing*, actually – even though I was still a shaky jelly inside.

And then, of course, there was Anna, who

had basically decided I was her best friend. She kept me a seat whenever we were in the same lessons.

In English she was mucking around next to me, quietly, so the teacher didn't see. She never seemed to worry about getting in trouble though.

She was drawing me silly pictures on Post-it notes and sticking them to my work and legs.

She took ages over one.

A dog.

No . . . a Gooner!

She was good at drawing, and it really did look like him – the same woolly-sheep fattiness. She'd guessed him exactly right.

Randomly.

That's my dog! I wrote underneath her picture. I started to write *psychic*, but I didn't know how to spell it, so I wrote: *Anna = mind-reader.*

She seemed to be another one of those girls like Lu who had X-ray eyes and could see into your brain.

'Ooh, mystic me,' she whispered, making her eyes go wide.

The teacher shook his head at her, so she pretended to write for a bit, but then began quietly picking out some old loom bands from the bottom of her pencil case.

She put a band round each of my pens, whispering that they were tiny friendship bracelets, and giggling.

No one had ever given me a friendship bracelet before – not ever.

And definitely not ones for all my pens.

Chapter 21

I couldn't believe how much the charm kept saving me. Dad hadn't let me down.

But still, I had to be super-careful that I didn't let *myself* down by letting any weirdness creep out to spoil everything. Like, on the way to the canteen with Anna at lunchtime, I was feeling so happy that I caught myself humming and singing under my breath.

I stopped myself before anyone noticed.

Un-weirding rule – Don't accidentally sing Mum's Story Sheep songs in public. Or ever.

Me and Anna got in the queue for chips. The place was SO rammed with kids, all barging past, it was getting me a bit nervy. I pulled my charm out . . . and straight away someone was tugging on my arm.

'Hey, Wood— I mean, Will!'

Kendall. With her face sun-beaming at me.

Crikes, this charm was like a Kendall magnet.

'Um, hi . . . er . .' I said, smiling like you're supposed to with new friends. I tried to think of something to say, hoping the charm would help me. But then Anna turned round and grinned at Kendall.

'Oh hi! I'm Anna. Who are you?'

They got chatting over me, so I didn't have to talk. I just stood there like a post, but they didn't seem to mind.

But then Casey came over too, and hovered next to Anna as well. I didn't look at her, but I went all twitchy again inside, still expecting her to bite my head off.

Except she totally ignored me. She just lurked there, her stodgy face all gormless, completely silent like before. Della hadn't trained her well at all. By herself Casey couldn't bully a fairy cake.

So there I was: Anna on one side, Kendall on the other. Both of them so charmed by me that they wanted me in the middle of them.

I felt like a charmer-boy sandwich.

And there was Casey: standing half out of the queue, by herself.

I was in, and she was out.

Who'd have guessed *that* would happen?

It felt GOOD.

Chapter 22

The charm even made PE okay.

PE!

My worst subject in the world.

I hated it, and it hated me.

I felt my belly tense as I walked into the boys' changing rooms. It was packed full of boys I didn't know, and there was no space for me to change. I clutched my charm and shuffled about near the doorway.

More awkwardness. I was just such an expert at it, even with a super-powered charm in my hand.

But then:

'Hey . . . you're that boy from the hairdresser's, aren't you?'

It was Josh.

Smiling at me, pulling on a sock.

I nodded, and he waved me over to him.

'All right?' he said. 'I thought it was you. Change here if you like.' And he moved his stuff up to make room.

Josh was making friends with me!

Cool Josh.

With ME.

And he'd hardly bothered with me at all in the hairdresser's – before I had the charm.

I got changed, clipping my charm firmly into my shorts pocket. Oh, I so needed it for THIS lesson.

We queued up at the hall door. Some of the boys were messing about, squashing their hands in their armpits to make farty noises. I'd never have dared to join in normally, but I had my charm and Josh next to me, so I started cracking my knuckles. I'd always been good at making

a LOUD crunching noise with my knuckles –
even though Mum hated me doing it and said
I'd give myself arthritis. Josh laughed and tried
to crack his knuckles too. Soon *everyone* was
trying to do it – but they all said I was the best
at it.

Then we had one of those early-in-the-term
PE lessons where we just played a bit of dodge
ball. Usually it'd have been like torture, and I'd
have stayed at the edges and never touched the
ball once. But with the charm in my pocket,
Josh and some others kept passing me the ball
– so it was okay and even a bit fun.

The words PE and fun in the same sentence.

Me and a boy like Josh being mates.

The charm had really turned my world upside
down.

It'd even got the birds on side. I'd seen TWO
magpies out the window in maths.

TWO happy ones.

Thanks, Dad.

Chapter 23

After school, me and Anna sat on the wall outside school while she texted her mum. The sun was warming me, and I was smiling on the inside at my day.

Then we walked along the road together until she had to turn off to meet her mum, and I was left by myself, walking amongst lots of kids.

I felt the old feeling creeping back. Shifty and awkward. My eyes darted around again, looking for Della.

I reached in my trouser pocket for my charm. It wasn't there.

My belly lurched.

It wasn't in my jacket pockets either.

WHERE WAS IT?

I was out in the street, surrounded by lots of school kids . . . *without my charm.* I'd LOST Dad's cube? No, NO!

Boom – my whole body filled to the brim with panic.

I'd had it when I was sitting on that wall with Anna. It had to be there!

I did a sharp swivel and sprinted back towards school.

But it was like the universe *knew* I was charm-less.

'Hey!'

A tennis ball came bouncing out of a garden right into my path. A boy in Hawthorn uniform waved at me over the wall to throw it back to him.

I didn't want to – I didn't have time! – but he was waiting. So I screeched to a halt, grabbed the ball and chucked it towards him. It wasn't a very high wall, but my Mr Bean arms made me do a duff throw, and it went completely the wrong way. It bounced off the gate post, and boinged back towards the road, straight on to the windscreen of a passing car, and then plopped straight into a deep, oily-looking puddle.

The car driver shouted at me through the glass, and I heard the boy swearing at me from the garden. Brilliant. I'd been without the charm for two minutes and everyone hated me already.

I hurried on, head down, through groups of kids. Then my phone went off in my trouser pocket – a text. I pulled it out – and, eww, an old apple core came out too.

I tossed it into a bus-stop bin as I passed.

But hang on, wait . . .

The apple was still in my hand.

I'd thrown my PHONE in the bin instead.

NOOO!

I scrabbled around in the rank rubbish, my face red. Where was it? The phone'd gone right down through old crisps packets and mouldy chips wrappers.

Un-weirding rule – Don't go bin-diving in the street. It's weird and totally charm-free.

But right then I didn't even care if anyone saw me. I had much more important things on my mind. I had to HURRY.

I finally found my phone right at the bottom of the bin and shot away up the street.

I ran back up to the wall me and Anna had been sitting on.

Please be there, cube!

And it was – lying in the grass behind.

Ahhhhh!

I held it against my cheek, breathing hard.

So that'd proved it, once and for all . . .

Un-weirding GOLDEN-EST rule – Don't lose Dad's charm, or you will fail at life. And never be able to face Dad again.

Chapter 24

I looked at my texts as I walked back along the road.

There were three from Nan.

THREE!

One saying she'd bought me an extra little present. Another one about something she'd seen on the telly. And then one saying she'd left a surprise for me at my house.

She'd been texting me all through the day!

Blimey, she really did like me a lot. And all this being liked was taking some getting used to.

I replied to Nan straight away in case she thought I was rude.

Then I headed for the shops.

Because I was a man with a plan. I'd made some new friends, but now I had some *serious* making-up to do with Lu. She'd still be spitting with me for ditching her and Kai this morning. I was going to have to try and melt her.

Or rather the charm was. After today, I knew I could rely on it.

In the Co-op I bought a big fat pack of iced buns to take round to Lu's house – her favourite. She finished school earlier than me now, so she'd already be home by this time. I wouldn't meet her and Kai in front of any Hawthorn kids – I was safe.

Then I felt so mean for thinking that that I grabbed another pack of buns. Sorry buns. Please-stay-friends-with-me buns. I bought some jelly babies too – to use as board game counters. Kai kept nicking Lu's ones for his games so nearly all her counters were lost in the sandpit or under the sofa.

I ran all the way to Lu's. I knocked on the door and went straight in. It was a tiny, ground-floor flat, but so noisy that if you waited for someone to hear the door you'd stand there until you were thirty-five.

Brits and Spears were having a barking party in the back bedroom, as usual. And I could see the back of Lu's mum's head in the lounge chair, the telly turned up loud. She hadn't noticed me, so I just crept through to Lu's room.

I stopped outside her closed door, chewing my lip. I put my ear against the door. Lu and Kai were in there.

Should I go in and be all sorry? No, that would definitely just annoy Lu more. I'd just act like nothing had happened, and let the charm do its stuff.

So I shoved the door open and ran in.

They were sitting on the bed, playing a beeping game on Lu's mum's tablet.

'PILE UP!' I yelled and threw myself on to the bed on top of them.

'Wooddddyyyy!' Kai squealed with delight.

He pummelled me with his tiny feet so I rolled off on to the floor.

'I'd have got here earlier, but I had to buy buns. And then I got jumped by a Darlek,' I said, lying on the carpet, grinning up at them. 'And then there was a sabre-toothed tiger at the bus stop, and . . .'

Uh-oh.

Lu was all blank-faced, like I wasn't even there.

Still, she wasn't telling me to GET OUT, which was a good-ish sign.

I put hand in my jacket pocket and gave the cube a rub.

'I bought some jelly babies too,' I blathered. 'If we tie strings to their bums, maybe we can use them to play *Mousie Mousie?*' Kai had lost all the pieces for that game as well.

I threw the sweet packet at Lu, hoping she'd laugh at that idea, but her cheek only flinched a tiny bit, as if an annoying fly had landed on it . . .

I took the cube right out of my pocket. Why

wasn't the cube working on Lu? Maybe she knew me too well, and it only charmed new people into being your friend?

'So . . . er . . .' I felt like all the puff had gone out of me now. I didn't know what to say. For a minute, it was tooth-achingly awkward.

Then, before I could stop him, Kai had bounced off the bed and snatched the cube out of my hand.

'No, Kai – that's *Woody*'s,' I said, nabbing it straight back off him.

'NAAA!' He screwed up his face and gritted his teeth at me like I'd just flushed his bear down the loo. 'NOOOO, WOODY!'

Now I'd upset him too – great. But he was easy to win round – no charm power needed.

I got down on all fours.

'Jump on, Kaiser Chief.'

'EEEEEEEE! Story Sheepppsssssssssss!' he cried, flinging himself at me.

He climbed on my back and started singing, while I turned into a demented sheep, throwing him off. He never got tired of it. Falling off and getting back on again, over and over again.

'Tired sheep,' I said after a bit, falling flat on my tummy.

'No, *more* bra bra!' cried Kai.

'Hey, but maybe the *very, very cool* sheeps is HUNGRY, Kai?' said Lu. It was the first thing she'd said since I'd arrived. But she'd said it in her quiet, dangerous voice.

And that bit about me being very, very cool . . .

I knelt up to try and work out what was going on.

Kai put his face close to mine, like he was inspecting me for sheep hunger. Then he patted me in a cute, worried way.

'Yesh . . . Get sheeps food,' he said, nodding seriously. Then he turned and waddled out the room.

'Uh? Sheeps food?' I asked, looking at Lu.

'I'd better go and see what he's doing,' she said with a smirk, and skipped out after him.

I followed them into the kitchen. Why couldn't the sheeps have eaten a nice iced bun? I had a horrid, sinking feeling that I was being set up. It'd be so like Lu.

Lu's mum waved and grinned at me over the loud telly as I passed through the lounge. I was a bit nervous of her, to be honest. She was all smiles whenever she saw me. But then in the next breath she'd tell Lu off for something, really snap-dragon fiercely. Hmm, I wondered where Lu got it from . . .

I closed the kitchen door behind me and Kai came running and leapt at me. It was only when he was in my arms that I realised he was holding some ham.

A very mucky piece that looked like it'd been sucked, dropped and used to blow his nose.

'Sheeps tea,' he said, and tried to stuff the ham into my mouth.

I turned my head away just in time so it slapped against my cheek. Ewwww.

'But Kai,' I said, through tight lips, keeping my face away from him. 'Sheep don't eat ham. They eat grass.'

Kai'd face dropped, like this was the worst

news he'd had for weeks. His lip started to wobble.

'I know, Kaisey-koo,' said Lu brightly. 'Let's make some grass sandwiches for the sheep!'

'Yesh!' He squirmed down out of my arms, and did one of his skippy-hoppy, happy dances on the spot. Then he stopped for a moment. 'And kwetchup?' he said, his head on one side.

'Yup,' said Lu, without missing a beat. Her eyes were shining under her fringe, like they did when she had an idea for a new prank. I knew I was in trouble. She was getting me back for ditching them this morning.

Kai was already out in the back garden pulling up handfuls of grass. Probably grass that Brits and Spears had weed on.

He came in waving a fat fistful at me, like I should be delighted.

'Sandwig for sheeps,' he yelled at the very top of his voice, even though the sheeps was standing right next to him.

Then I watched them make me the most disgusting sandwich in the whole of history.

159

They squelched in lots of ketchup on top of the grass, then some jam and some squirty cheese from a tube. And to finish it off, Lu emptied in one of her mum's powdered soup sachets.

She put it on a plate and handed it to Kai.

'Ooh, yum, yum – lucky sheeps,' said Lu. 'He'd better eat it all up.'

Kai brought me the sandwich, his face lit up. Lu was sniggering. She knew I couldn't say no to him.

I took a tiny bite while Kai watched with massive eyes. It was stringy, gritty and squelchy all at the same time. Ugh. A huge blob of ketchup and jam plopped out the side and dribbled all down my new jacket from Nan, which I hadn't got round to taking off.

I pretend-nibbled more of the sandwich, making lots of yummmmmeee noises for Kai. He whooped and clapped for a while, but I knew he'd get bored of playing Very-Hungry-Sheeps before long. And sure enough, he soon started a new game of whirling a tea towel and shouting tummy-buuuuuummy out the back door. Kai liked saying rhymes, or rather *shouting* rhymes – often accidentally rude ones. Another reason why I had to hide from them in the street if my un-weirding plan was going to work.

I dropped my sarnie into the bin when his back was turned.

'Thanks for that,' I said to Lu under my breath, but making sure to smile too, so she knew I was only joking.

She gave me the tiniest smile back.

'You're welcome,' she said. 'Oh, and you've got a tiny dot of something just there,' she added, pointing to the massive splodge of ketchup on my coat. 'On your cool new stuff.'

But then she grinned. Kind of friendly-ish.

I smiled too.

I'd had to work hard, but we were all right again. More or less.

Even though she was taking the mickey out of my clothes.

Even though she'd just got me covered in sheep's food on purpose.

But crikey, it could wear me out, all this.

Having to be old weirdy Woody to keep Lu on side, and then swapping to charming William for my new mates.

It was like being two people all at once.

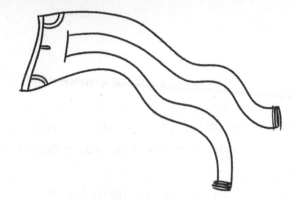

Chapter 25

I went to see Dad again before I went home.

Just to say thank you.

Thank you times about five billion.

Then I scooted home.

I closed the front door behind me when I got home and breathed out. Ahhhh. I knew Mum was out doing a kiddies' party, so the house would be nice and quiet.

Or not.

As I stepped into the hall, there was a huge noise like an elephant farting. What had happened to my text alert?

Lu had happened to it, of course.

Well, okay, I probably deserved it.

All the din made Shaun shuffle out the kitchen – with Gooner next to him, wag-wag-wagging at me.

'It was just my phone misbehaving,' I said. 'It's gone loud.'

'Oh yes, they do that,' said Shaun. 'All by themselves – it's like they're bewitched.' Then he grinned and looked at me hard. So he DID know we'd messed with his phone.

'Er, yeah,' I said, looking away quickly.

'So how was school then?' he said. He eyed my mucky jacket. 'Eventful?'

I shrugged. I usually did this instead of speaking to Shaun.

But he nodded like I'd answered him, and pointed behind him into the kitchen.

'Your grandma left some cakes on the door-step for you. And then Mum made you one too.'

I hurried into the kitchen to look. On the table was a posh bakery-shop cake box with a note: *I hope you enjoyed your first day at school today, William. Celebrate! Luv Babs* x

The box was full of gooey cupcakes with thick blue icing and sweets on top. They were literally Mum's worst E-numbery, sugary nightmare. Once Kai dropped some jelly sweets on the lawn, and our ducks ate them and did rainbow poo. Mum made a huge fuss even about THEM eating E-numbers – and they eat poo and slugs.

Next to the box was one of Mum's brown, stodgy organic date-and-walnut cakes – the kind she made with apple juice instead of sugar – with a scrawly note on the back of an envelope. *Hope you had a happy day, Woods. See you later! Love Mum xx*

I picked a corner off Mum's cake. It was still warm like she'd only just baked it. Did she make her cake *after* Nan's arrived?

Was Mum trying to have a CAKE-OFF with Nan?

I turned and gawped at Shaun, who was filling the kettle at the sink. He just raised one eyebrow and shrugged his shoulders in a don't-look-at-me kind of way.

'I'd just eat them if I were you,' he said.

I nodded. It seemed like a good idea. The cakes were confusing me.

'Want some?' I mumbled.

'Ta.' He grinned and shuffled over with a plate. I was so sure he'd go for Mum's organic cake, but he grabbed one of Nan's neon sugar-poison ones instead.

He took a huge bite.

'These are pretty nice, eh?' he said, chewing.

I stared at him in surprise. He had some blue icing in his beard.

Now he was confusing me too. And he'd better wash that icing off his face before Mum saw, or he'd probably have to sleep in the duck house in E-number disgrace.

I put one of Nan's cakes and a slice of Mum's on a plate.

William cake. Woody cake.

I even had two different *CAKE* lives now?

Phew. I needed an early night.

I was *done in*.

Chapter 26

As I went downstairs the next morning I was a bit less scared about school.

A *bit* less.

I'd be okay, wouldn't I, as long as I remembered three things:

1. Follow my rules to keep my weirdness in.
2. Keep my William and Woody lives apart.
3. KEEP DAD'S CHARM WITH ME ALL THE TIME!!!

I'd visit Dad again on the way to school too.

Just to double-check he was still *with me*. Still making his charm work for me.

But I'd better hurry. I pulled on my jacket and opened the fridge for some milk. Mum had made my lunch again – she'd left it in the fridge with a note. And it was another pongy weirdy delight. A mung-beansprout, tofu and spring onion rice thing, left over from dinner.

Sorry Mum, but no ta . . .

I scrapped it into Gooner's bowl and he got his woolly head straight in the trough – good lad.

Then I slurped some milk from a carton, and grabbed a lump of Mum's cake to take with me. Nan's really were too sickly for breakfast. I patted my pocket for my charm, and zipped out the back door so Mum didn't hear.

On my way out I kaboomed the school for luck. And touched lots of wood – both the gate and the apple tree. It was more out of habit though. I didn't need any luck – not now I had Dad's charm.

I scoffed down the cake and ran. There were

some Hawthorn kids about so I pulled up my hood so they didn't see that the sprinting-in-the-wrong-direction kid was me.

I got to Dad's grave in three minutes twenty seconds.

I ran straight up to it and hugged it. Without even thinking what I was doing.

And then jumped back, looking around in case anyone was watching me. No one was, luckily.

Un-weirding rule – Don't hug gravestones, even if they are your own dad's.

'Hi Dad . . . it's me again, William.'

I *was* William too – I really had done it. Everyone called me that now!

'Still gonna need lots of help again today. Thank you and please.'

I laid the cube on top of the gravestone – like he might turbo-charge it.

DONG!

The church bells. Quarter past eight. Time to go.

I patted the stone, and scooted back out of the graveyard, feeling bouncier.

I'd taken LITERALLY three steps when:

'Hey Wood—. Er . . . I mean, Will!'

Kendall *again*? Did she live near here or something?

She crossed the road to me, looking pink-cheeked. 'Hi! Can I walk with you?'

I nodded and remembered to smile.

Then we walked along together a little way, not speaking, until there was a sudden scream behind us.

'KENDYYYY!' We were stampeded by some girls I didn't know, but all in our uniform. Girls like that usually ignored me – like I was a boring nothing. But now they surrounded us, all staring right at me. They were blocking the pavement so that some older school kids swore at us and stepped into the road to get by. And what a racket they were making – everyone in the street was looking over.

Girls-Aloud.

Girls A-Very-*Very*-Loud.

Kendall started shrieking too. And she used to be one the quietest girls I knew.

It was a bit much, but I grasped the charm and said hi as friendly as I could. Then:

'So who's your boyf, Kendy?' said one of her friends.

WHAT?!

No, no, no!

I put my head down and walked away from them, trying to be calm, trying not to actually run. But they followed me. Whispering and giggling. I kept hearing my name: Will, William.

My face was on fire, and I was starting to sweat.

And then it got even worse.

'Hey, Will?' one of the girls called at my back. I half-turned and then wished I hadn't. 'Kendall thinks you're fit. She thinks you look like Robbie Mars!'

Kendall screamed and gave her friend a shove into the wall, and the others all hooted with laughter.

Argh!

Now there must be actual flames coming out of my cheeks.

I walked on even faster.

The charm was working over-time! It was like Dad really had turbo-charged it today. It was making Kendall like me much, MUCH too much. I suddenly wished it had an on/off switch.

Lu's words popped into my head: *Kendall's gone boy-mad*.

So now she was mad on ME? I glanced behind. Kendall was at the front, her face the colour of a postbox. She caught my eye and gave me a shy smile.

Like she *loved* me or something.

OVERLOAD!

We were just by the old shops parade. I turned and pushed through the nearest shop door. Without stopping to check which door it was.

I was right inside before I realised it was the nail varnish and make-up shop.

Oh.

No.

What a ginormous idiot.

Un-weirding rule – Don't make yourself part of a beauty parlour's window display.

I whipped round, ready to run out again, but the girls were right outside, waving at me through the glass.

I was being chased by girls again. But this time because they LIKED me. This had NOT been in my plan.

I stayed where I was, blushing from head to foot.

But the shop door had made a bell ring, and a lady appeared from behind the screen and looked me up and down in surprise.

'Sorry, we're not quite open yet, love,' she said. 'Can I help?'

I blinked at her, desperately trying to think of something to say, but no words came. I wanted to leg it, but out the corner of my eye, I could see one of Kendall's mates drawing two big hearts on the dewy glass.

So I just stood there, um-ing and er-ing, pretending to look at a leaflet on the counter.

Eyelash dying – £12
Eyebrows threading – £14
What did any of it even *mean*?

The make-up lady's own eyebrows were right up in her hair. They were just strange, thin lines like Nan's – like someone had drawn them on with a felt-pen. Maybe that's what threading meant.

I was way out of my depth. But I carried on staring at the leaflet and nodding like I was concentrating hard on reading it.

Sorry lady – please talk to me for two more minutes.

'Er, so would you like an appointment?' she asked. She pressed her lipsticky lips together and looked at me. 'Or . . . ?'

No, lady!

I took another peek over my shoulder. The girls had finally gone. Oh joy.

'No! Sorry . . . oops, wrong shop. Sorry, sorry,' I said, stuffing the leaflet back into the holder, so it got all crumpled.

I flew out the door.

Where were they?

I stood flat against the wall and peered. Ah, there – up the road. Far enough away.

I leant against the wall, breathing.

I felt like I'd only *just* survived. THAT was off the scale.

Dad had probably liked that much attention, but I wasn't used to it.

Maybe I was a beginner charmer, and I just needed more practice.

Hopefully.

Chapter 27

But then the day carried on like that.

FULL ON.

The charm was doing great, but I wasn't. All the liking was becoming very hard to handle. I had to hide in the loos TWICE at break time to avoid Kendall and her Girls-A-Very-Loud.

I'm sure Dad never hid from girls in loos.

Even Nan was getting a bit too much. When I looked at my phone once in the loo, I had three more texts from her, about random stuff. She was texting me ALL the time. For my whole life I hadn't had a nan . . . and now suddenly I had a 24/7, *round-the-clock* nan.

Thank goodness for Anna – she was charmed by me, but in a nice, easy way. She was basically my lifesaver.

We went everywhere we could together. At lunchtime we went to the canteen for our chips. It was so busy in there, and people weren't queuing properly. The crush was getting me jumpy – too many people all at once. I got out my cube, but then I thought I saw Kendall across the hall so I dropped it straight back into my pocket and hid behind Josh. I didn't want to magnet her. Not after this morning.

I was in the middle of Anna and Josh in the queue, like a charmer-boy sandwich again. And of course, Casey was there too, Siamese-twinning herself to Anna, but I hardly even noticed her any more.

But then I saw Josh look at her and roll his eyes.

I watched him edge his feet backwards so Casey had to step right back.

Half pushing her out of the queue.

On purpose.

Okay . . .

Yeah, meh to her!

So I shuffled back too, making Casey scuffle back even more.

Now she wasn't in the queue at all.

I was IN – with Josh – and she was OUT, same as yesterday.

But this time she was right, *right* out. As far as I wanted to push her.

Josh saw what I'd done and winked at me.

I waited to feel good about that.

But then somehow I didn't.

Chapter 28

The day was seeming very long.

And then in the afternoon we had double science too. Mank.

Anna sat next to me. She spotted the cube-charm in my pencil case, and had a mess-around with it. But then she handed it back to me just as the teacher, Mr Withington, was looking over. He raised an eyebrow at me, but didn't say anything.

Then at the end of the lesson, I was just piling out the classroom with everyone else when: 'William – can I have a quick word?' Mr

Withington was sitting on the edge of his desk, waggling his finger at me to come over.

'Sir?'

'Nice Rubik's Cube you got there,' he said.

My heart leapt into my throat. I hung my head, blushing, trying not to let tears start in my eyes. I completely hated getting told off.

I felt for the charm in my pocket. Could it charm angry teachers? No, I didn't have a hope.

'So . . . I just wanted to ask you, was your dad called William Trindle?'

Uh?

I looked straight at him then.

'Er, yeah!'

But . . . *how* did he know?!

'Ah, thought so. I was at school with him,' he said, stroking down his beard.

'You went to school with my dad? HERE?' I said.

'Yep, right here,' he smiled. 'I know, eh? I keep trying to leave, but I'm having too much fun . . . or *something*.'

My head was buzzing.

'But, how did you know it was *me* . . . ?' I began.

'How? Well, your name was a huge clue!' he laughed. 'And you're the spit of him back then. And the Rubik's Cube jogged my memory too. I remember your dad was a whizz at those.'

'So . . . were you friends with my dad at school, sir?' My face went hot. I wouldn't have dared to ask Mr Withington questions normally, but I felt really nosey about this.

'Oh, noooo, he was way too cool to bother with the likes of me.'

Oh. I suddenly thought about when me and Josh had pushed Casey out of the lunch queue on purpose. I guess being popular and charming *could* go to your head. Or even put you on a bully team if you weren't careful. I felt a bit dazed. But Mr Withington was still talking.

'It was such an awful shame what happened – the accident and everything . . .' His voice trailed off, as he straightened a chair with his foot. 'But, *anyway* – here YOU are,' he said. A little smile. 'Playing around in my class.'

Uh-oh. I looked back at my feet and gritted my teeth. Was the telling-off part coming now?

I put my hands deeper into my pockets and held the charm tighter.

'But actually, your under-table Rubik's-cubing gave me an idea. Are you quick at doing them?'

I did a tiny nod.

'Right, so here's the thing.' He pointed his finger at me. 'I've rounded up some kids to do some stuff at the New Parents' Evening tonight. The head likes to put on a few short skits in between all the talking – kids doing music, singing and stuff – so the parents don't fall asleep. But one person has just dropped out on me. You up for it? I'm kind of desperate, so you'll be helping me out. I thought you could do a Rubik's Cube Grand Challenge. Maybe against the clock to add a bit of drama?'

BE IN A SHOW?

Oh, no way, not *ever*!

But how could I say no to a teacher? So I half-shook my head and half-nodded, which came out as an odd head-whirling move.

'Or . . . I'm thinking on my feet now . . .' he said, tugging his beard, '. . . how about we do a Rubik's Cube RACE, you and me? Might be fun. You'll beat me, no problem – and the kids'll love that!'

A RACE? *What?!* I wouldn't even be able to stay standing up . . .

But of course, I just did another dumb head-whirl.

'Great!' He patted my shoulder and started walking off across the classroom, like it was all arranged. 'You'll have the audience eating out of your hand – like your dad always did. A right show-man, he was.'

Er . . . or more like I'll cry or wet myself, and the audience will point and laugh.

Mr Withington pulled open a cupboard door.

'I'm sure there are some cubes in this cupboard *somewhere*. But you'd best get off to your next lesson now. If you can get to the hall by seven thirty, that'd be great.'

I gawped. Had I somehow *agreed*?

But he was already crouching down, pulling

stuff out of the cupboard, so there was nothing to do but scuttle away.

How had I let this happen?

Me on an actual stage. With loads of eyes looking at me . . .

I HAD to dodge out of it. I just couldn't do it.

Mr Withington said Dad had loved being on stage and charming a crowd. But not stupid me. Not even with the charm.

Being like Dad was turning out to be harder than I'd thought.

And I wasn't really coping with being charming, was I? Not AT ALL.

Dad was helping me with his charm, but I was getting more and more afraid that I might let him down.

There was nothing for it – I'd just have to pretend to be ill tonight.

It was lie or die.

Chapter 29

I walked out of school with Anna, feeling like I needed to lie down forever, after all that being popular.

And now I had this horrid show to think about.

'Wassup, duck?' said Anna. 'That's what my mum says when I have a face like yours.' And she pulled a wonky face at me.

'I'm okay. Really!' I gave her a big smile. She was so confident; I didn't want to tell her I was wussing about being in a show. She'd never understand.

A car had drawn up at the kerb right by us. Nan.

She was *following me around* now?

'Hiya, darling! I thought I'd come and treat you to a drive-through from Bingz?' she called through the car window over her music. 'What d'you say? I'm sure you're hungry! My Will was ALWAYS starving after school. Your friend can come too, if you like?'

'Um . . . ok, thanks . . .'

I turned to Anna with a shrug. 'Do you wanna come? That's my nan,' I said. At least Nan's car wasn't embarrassingly weird.

'Ah no, I can't. I've got to go to the chemist and the shops for Mum,' sighed Anna, as I opened the car door and got in. 'But thank you!'

We drove off with a wave.

Bingz burger place was only down the road, but I'd never even been there before. A boy in my class once had his birthday party there and I got invited – the whole class was – but Mum hadn't let me go. She hated the place, cos she was so organic-ish. Lu said that Mum and Shaun only ate nuts and carrots that people had been kind to, and Bingz didn't have any of those.

But I was interested to see what it was like. Mum would never know.

'Do you know what you want, babe?' Nan asked, as she pulled off next to the big red BINGZ sign.

'Er, maybe fries?' I said. 'Thank you.'

Nan nodded, and turned to talk to a girl through the window. 'I got you fries,' she said, turning back to me. 'Plus a cheeseburger and a chocolate milkshake for good measure . . . Those were William's absolute faves.'

'Um, thanks.'

Oh no, but would it be a *beef* burger? I'd forgotten to tell her I was vegetarian.

Too late – she was already driving to another window. Another girl leant out and handed her my food – it was ready *already?*

Nan handed me a huge, freezy cup of milkshake, and put a warm paper bag on my lap.

She drove towards the exit as I unwrapped my food.

Yep, the burger was definitely meat. Argh, what could I *do*?! I had to try and eat it. Nan had spent *even more* money on me.

And it was Dad's favourite.

I sniffed it.

It smelt a bit like Gooner's food.

Dad had liked this?

I held my breath and took a tiny nibble bite, trying hard not to think of the cows in the field at the edge of town with their sweet, furry faces. But the more I tried not to think about them, the more I did, and I nearly gagged.

Somehow I turned it into a sort-of cough, and Nan didn't seem to notice.

'Yummy?' she asked, her eyes on the traffic, trying to pull out.

'Mmmm,' I nodded, the lump of burger still on my tongue.

One, two, three . . . I did a big, gulpy swallow and took the burger down. Then I quickly sucked on the milkshake to take the taste away. At least that was nice – it tasted like melted ice cream.

But I just couldn't eat any more burger.

I know normal people went mad for food like this – people like Dad – but I couldn't make myself.

I got out my mobile and pretended to look at a text which wasn't there.

'Um . . . er . . . sorry, Nan-I-mean-Babs. Mum's just texted to say I have to go home, cos I've got an appointment thingy,' I stuttered, knowing I was flushing pink.

Just let me out of this car soon, so I can bin this dog-food burger without you seeing!

'Oh, so your mother texts you on your new phone, then?' Nan said, with an edge to her voice.

Oops. I'd forgotten that Nan knew Mum hated mobile phones.

'Um . . . well, not exactly,' I gabbled. 'Only if it's an emergency. I mean, not that today's appointment is an emergency, but . . .' Ugh, I was going to dig myself a massive crater with all this fibbing.

But Nan just nodded. 'S'okay. I'll drop you

off now. Oh, and I've got you a couple of little extra pressies. They're in that red plastic bag on the back seat.'

I reached behind me and nabbed the bag.

There was a big bag of sweets in there, and this bottle of spray stuff.

Aftershave?

'Um . . . thanks,' I said.

But I wasn't even twelve yet – not for three weeks. And I never used any bathroom stuff like that. Mum had got me this natural nettle-and-sage deodorant from the health food shop in the summer, but I hadn't used it cos it made me smell like a weird plant.

Nan pulled into the bus stop again at the end of our road, and took the bottle from my hand.

'It's such a lovely smell,' she said. 'I got it for you because it's the exact same brand Will used.'

She took the lid off and sprayed a bit on my arm.

Cor, it was strong stuff! It filled the car like a fog and made my eyes sting.

Nan was quiet. She was just staring into space,

nodding. It looked like the spray had made her eyes sting too.

That was when a penny suddenly dropped in my brain.

I knew Nan wanted me to be like Dad.

But now I saw something else too – she actually wanted to pretend I WAS him.

Pretend he was alive again.

And how did I deal with THAT?

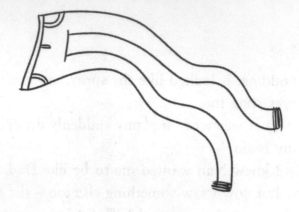

Chapter 30

What a day. It'd felt like a year.

I was so glad that Mum and Shaun weren't there when I got in. I was wiped out, and so done with being charming William. I just wanted to hide away and be weirdy Woody again for a bit. Indoors. By myself.

But Gooner had other ideas. He bounced up to me with his ropey toy. Then he stood and scratched on the door, desperate for his after-school walkies.

'Okay, okay, I s'pose I'll *have* to take you out,' I sighed. 'I don't *want* to, so it's a good job I love you. And look what I've got!'

I plopped the spongy burger roll into the bin. Then I made Gooner sit-and-shake-a-paw, and fed him the burger. His eyes went all wide in amazement and joy, and he gulped it down in one go. Gone.

'You're such a hoglet,' I said, grabbing a lead. I double-checked my pocket to make sure the charm was there, and we went back out the door.

I wasn't planning on going far – just round the block, very fast, so I didn't have to see ANYONE.

I had my eyes peeled the whole way. Which is why halfway down the street next to ours, I spotted Anna in the distance, walking along towards me with two shopping bags.

I whirled round and went the other way before she saw me. I really liked Anna, but I couldn't face any more having-to-be-charming now.

But *what?* . . .

Coming the OTHER WAY was LU. Still a way off. Pushing Kai in a pushchair. She'd obviously just picked him up from the childminder's.

I'd have known it was them with my eyes closed because, even at this distance, I could hear Kai shouting one of his loud rhymes – something like wooeeee shooeee pooeeeee.

I turned one way and then other, but there were no side roads to go down – and I suddenly realised: I was going to get caught in the middle of them!

And WHO would I be then – Woody or Willliam?

PANIC!

I raced over and crouched between two parked cars, tucked in out the way of any traffic, yanking Gooner's lead so he stayed close to me. I got out my charm and held it against my cheek. I'd just wait here and let Anna and Lu go past. Then walkies over – home. Safe.

But:

'Oi, William – what you doing down there?'

One of Kendall's Girls-A-Very-Loud mates was in the bus stop over the road, with some other girl who was sniggering.

Perfect.

Why hadn't I noticed them there? Or had they just come out of a house?

I stood up with a start, banging my knee on a car bumper. Then I did some seriously rubbish acting, pretending to inspect the car's headlight like I was suddenly an eleven-year-old car mechanic. Doh. I waved awkwardly and walked back to the pavement.

'Where's Kendall?' called the Girl-A-Very-Loud. Then she started singing:

'Kendy and Will sitting in a tree . . . K-I-S-S-I-N-G.'

WHAT?

OMG – this was literally like being stuck in a NIGHTMARE.

I looked this way and that. What could I do? I couldn't hide again. The bus-stop girls would see. And Anna and Lu were still coming. Lu had stopped to sort Kai out, and Anna was walking slowly looking down at her phone. But they were getting closer.

There was no way out. I was trapped on all sides.

ARGGHHH!

My heart started drumming faster.

It felt like the two worlds I'd been trying to keep apart were about to *crash*, squash me in the middle, and FINISH ME OFF.

I wanted to turn into a flea on Gooner's back and disappear.

Then . . . . rescue!

A bus came along, blocking the girls at the bus stop.

It was my chance!

I dived head first into a bushy, over-hanging hedge next to me, dragging Gooner with me.

Obviously I was getting to be an expert at hedge-hiding – but this one was the worst yet. It was that thick, spiky kind, made out of those fir trees that smelt like Christmas. It was scratching me up, but I squashed myself into it as far as I could get, my heart crashing in my chest. Gooner was half in the bush too, but his tail was sticking out. I reached down and pulled his bum right round so he was standing under the branches.

But he wasn't helping at all. He was straining on his lead, panting excitedly. And his tail was wagging so much it was making the branches wobble.

I could hear footsteps. The girls were nearly here!

'No, stop it!' I whispered to him, my voice squeaking with panic. 'Sit!' But of course, he wouldn't, cos I didn't have a dog treat to give him.

I blame Gooner for what happened next.

A car hooted loudly, making me leap out of my skin. I peered out between the branches and saw a lady pointing at me through her car window. I tried to ignore her. But she wound the window down further and yelled at me to stop destroying her hedge and to GET OUT NOW.

So I stepped out, covered with bits of twig, my face red hot, muttering *sorry*. The lady glared and drove off fast, leaving me standing in the street.

Right in the middle of Anna and Lu.

SPLAT.

The bus had gone too, but the Girl A-Very-Loud and her friend hadn't got on it. They were gazing over at me in open-mouthed delight – like watching me being told off for hiding in a hedge had been the best show they'd seen in ages. I was surprised they hadn't got popcorn.

'William?' Anna had put down her bags and was staring at me. She wasn't smiling. 'What were you doing in that hedge?'

I just looked at her, frozen to the spot. I had no words. Nothing. If she'd guessed I was hiding from her, she'd hate me . . .

I could feel Lu's eyes on me from the other side. Cold, cold eyes.

I dared a peek towards her. And OMG, her face. I caught my breath like I'd been punched in the gut. I could tell she *definitely* knew I'd been hiding from her.

'WOODYYYYYY!' cried Kai, leaning out of his pushchair so far that his hair nearly touched the ground. 'Hide-n-sick?' He covered his face with his little hands.

Yep, great. Thanks, Kai. Just in case anyone was unclear.

'*Woody?*' said Anna. 'Is that your nickname or something?'

I half-nodded. Then Lu made an odd squeaking noise, so I changed the nod to a shake.

The bus-stop girls were singing their kissing song again.

Too much, TOO MUCH. I felt light-headed, and my heart seemed to be beating in my throat. Maybe I was having an actual heart attack.

'What's all this *William* business?' Lu hissed. 'Have you changed your NAME *too*?' Her eyes were drilling into me, and she was jerking the pushchair towards me like she wanted to run me over.

I rubbed my arm across my sweaty forehead and half-nodded.

'Er, no, well, yeah . . .' I stammered.

'William,' Lu said, quietly. She was scratching her arm so much I was sure she'd make it bleed. 'Will.I.Am. Like that stupid rapper bloke off the telly who thinks he's really it,' she said in a low, tight voice. 'THINKS he is,' she said, getting louder.

Anna laughed, like Lu had just made a joke.

But it wasn't a joke.

OH NO.

Lu was being mean. Meaner than she'd ever been to me in her life.

And Anna was laughing cos she was on Lu's side now. Because she was angry with me too.

'So are you a friend from William's old school then?' Anna asked Lu. 'Like Casey?

No, no! Don't mention CASEY.

But it was done.

'Oh Will.I.Am's friend, *Casey*?' Lu's eyes were slits, her face dark with hating me. Brilliant – so now she thought I'd was matey with Casey too. Just to add to my many crimes.

That was it. I was going to go and cry in a hole forever.

You'd think it couldn't have got any worse. But who should come along then – just to put the icing on the poo cake that was my afternoon?

Mum.

On her way home, in her Story Sheep van.

She pulled up and wound down her window. Everyone turned to look at her. To stare.

At least she wasn't dressed as a sheep, but I could see straight away from her face that she was narky, and about to tell me off in front of everyone. She never worried about stuff like that. Stuff like completely *embarrassing* me into the ground.

'Woods!' she snapped. 'Did you know it's the New Parents' Evening tonight? I got an email from your school today, asking me if I was coming, because I hadn't responded to their letter.'

I grimaced sorry. Even though I hadn't told her on purpose – the invite letter was hidden in my locker where she'd never find it.

'And the email said you're part of the *show* tonight too?' She said 'show' like she couldn't believe it.

I shook my head hard.

'Well, the email says you are, Woody – so you ARE! Be home *soon*!' Then she just drove off.

'That's your mum?' said Anna. I was sure she said it in *a what?-that-weird-woman-in-that-weird-van?* kind of a tone.

I did a tiny nod.

So now Anna hated me for hiding from her, AND she knew the truth about my weirdness.

Everything was ruined.

My misery was complete.

But . . . WHY wasn't my charm helping me?

Dad! I NEED SO MUCH HELP RIGHT NOW.

I felt in my pocket for my cube.

But it wasn't there. Or in the other one.

NO, NO! Surely I hadn't lost it *again*.

I'd only had it a few minutes ago . . .

I flung down Gooner's lead and pushed my way back into the hedge I'd been in, scrabbling in the muddy leaves underneath it with my fingers. Not even caring that I was being weird.

No cube.

I rubbed my hot face with my mucky hands.

I could feel my tears starting.

This was totally the final straw. I was going

to crack up. I rushed over to where I'd been crouching behind the cars.

And there it was in the road.

The cube.

Dad's precious charm . . .

Run over on the tarmac.

Shattered.

Broken into a million shiny, golden pieces.

I scooped some up into my hand, as a huge, juddering sob came up through me. Then I turned and legged it.

I didn't even stop to grab Gooner.

Chapter 31

I looked down at the broken mess in my palm as I ran.

The cube was a total goner.

And without it, so was I.

Charmless forever.

School and my whole life would be HELL on a stick now, because, of course, my new friends *only* liked me because they were charmed.

And now I didn't even have Lu any more.

I ACTUALLY HAD NO FRIENDS AT ALL.

I slowed to a walk, put my hood up and

slumped along, just going anywhere as long as it was away.

And I'd even abandoned Gooner. I knew Lu would probably drop him off at my house. But I couldn't go home for hours – Mum'd just get on at me about the show. And I certainly couldn't go to Nan's now I'd broken the charm.

I was basically homeless.

And now it was raining.

I was getting so worked up that I wasn't looking where I was going. I nearly bumped into a lady, but swerved at the last minute, skidding on a crisp packet right in front of her. I stuttered apologies and did a little sorry wave, and somehow managed to poke myself in the eye.

The lady gave me a strange look and hurried past. I didn't blame her. What a weirdy no-hoper I was.

So much for un-weirding. My natural weird-ness would always find its way out. I wasn't even going to BOTHER with my un-weirding rules any more. There was no point.

I bit my lip, battling my tears. Stomping down streets I didn't know.

A car pulled up just ahead of me, and a kid ran out of a house and got in.

'Hi, Dad!' he said, slamming the door.

Dad . . .

The word hit me in the chest.

Making me think of the one thing I was trying NOT to think about.

The worst thing of all.

I could NEVER go and see Dad again.

I'd broken his charm.

His precious charm that he'd lent me.

He'd tried to help me, but I hadn't coped with being charming. I just couldn't hack it.

My tears came flooding then.

I was a rubbish son.

Chapter 32

I was sobbing my heart out in the street. People were staring.

I needed to hide, and I was near the park, so I scurried in. No one was about, only a few joggers, and I could go in that baby house where I saw that girl that time. It'd be dry in there, at least.

That girl . . . The one who nearly liked me until I blew it. Obviously.

But the baby house turned out to be another one of my many bad ideas. I was just ducking down to go in the tiny door when I heard a shout.

'Will?'

One of the joggers was waving at me.

Who was it? I squinted through the rain.

JOSH!

Cool, un-weird Josh. A boy who'd definitely never *ever* cry in a baby house.

He was jogging over to me.

No, go away! Not now.

I didn't even have my charm any more, so I couldn't even hope to be saved by that.

I stared at my shoes, and wiped my teary face on my sleeve, but I knew it was hopeless.

'Hey! What you doing, mate?' he said, as he came through the gate into the playground.

'Um . . .'

Good question. What WAS I doing?

Just blubbing in a little kids' playground in the rain. As you do.

'Er, I was . . . er . . . looking for something,' I said.

Josh looked all around on the ground, where there was obviously NOTHING. Because I'd lied.

'Oh. What did you lose?' he asked.

He didn't say: why were you even in this playground in the first place, Toddler Face? But I knew he was thinking it.

'Er, nothing much,' I said, quickly. Then in a whisper, 'Well, just my best friend, and al—'

I stopped mid-word.

Josh had heard me. Even his ears were sharp.

He was staring at me hard, looking confused.

'Are you *all right*, man?'

I nodded and did a big smile like I was, of course, *definitely* completely okay. But it didn't really work.

Josh shuffled his feet awkwardly. He scuffed a stone with his toe.

'Well . . . okay, man. I'll let you get on then . . . Laters.'

He did a half-hearted high-five in the air, swivelled and jogged back over to the gate.

Clearly embarrassed by me.

And there it was again: another friend gone.

Josh'd be pushing ME out of the lunch queue now.

I waited until he was out of sight and then dived inside the baby house, whacking my head as I went.

Owwww!

I sat in a huddle with my jumper over my knees, and cried some more.

See, Dad, you needed a son like *Josh*. Not me, the BIG weirdy fail.

I was shivering. The rain was getting through a small hole in the roof and plopping on me in freezing drips.

Even better: a *drippy* baby house.

But I was in the right place, because I really did feel about two years old.

Chapter 33

'Woods?'

I jumped.

I was still hugging my knees in the little house, frozen. Maybe I'd dozed off a bit. How long had I been in there?

It was Lu, peeping through the low door.

Lu.

The last person I expected to see ever.

And another face . . . Anna!

And then Gooner too, who rushed in, wagging for England. Friends with me straight away.

I hugged his warm, damp head.

Oh, my Gooner boy.

'H-h-ow . . . how did you find me?' I
mumbled. My eyes felt swollen, and I felt foggy-
brained, like I wasn't quite awake.

'Josh,' said Anna. 'I went round to Lu's for
a chat, and he texted me to say you were here.
So we came.'

I shook my head, trying to understand.

Had they come to yell at me?

And why had Josh texted her? To tell her I
was a big, crying joke in a baby house?

They squashed in either side of me, sand-
wiching me between them. Except I wasn't a
charmer-boy sandwich this time: *that* sandwich
was in the BIN now.

Gooner still had his head on my lap. I patted
him and didn't look at the girls.

'We came to see if you were all right,' said
Anna. 'Josh was worried cos he said you seemed
pretty upset.'

Josh had said that?

And Lu'd wanted to come to find me. *Really?*

I looked at Lu – and she did a tiny, embarrassed nod.

'Anna explained some stuff,' she said with a shrug. 'She told me how you've got stuck with Casey at school.' She shook her head. 'It's hard to believe: *Casey* the cling-on.'

'Except I said that secondary school IS pretty scary at the start,' said Anna, 'and you'll do anything to make new friends.'

I looked at Anna, surprised. How would SHE know that?

'Hmmm,' Lu said, and gave me one of her X-ray looks. 'And Josh said you were sad cos you'd lost your best friend.'

Ah, so Josh really HAD heard me muttering. Lu traced the pattern of her coat with her finger. She knew I'd meant her.

'I've been grumpy with you, haven't I? Enough to make you *hide* from me!' She half-laughed, but kept her eyes down. 'It's just . . . I didn't like it when you started getting all cool and grown up. I understand now: you were just trying to fit in, but . . . I thought you wanted to leave me behind.'

A red dot appeared in the middle of her cheek, and when she turned to me, her eyes looked shiny wet.

'Sorry,' she whispered. 'And you haven't lost me. I'm still here. You big wally!'

Well, that set me off again too. Tears filled my eyes so I couldn't see out.

There was a pause while I sniffed, gulped and nodded.

'Well . . . *I'm* sorry too. I've been kind of losing the plot since I started Hawthorn.'

Anna budged me with her shoulder.

'Well, lost plot or not, you're my only real friend at school so far. Just so you know.'

'What, weirdo me?' I said, sighing. ' Are you sure?'

She tutted and laughed. And then I did too. Even I could hear that I sounded like Eeyore.

'Yeah, I'm sure,' she said. 'I like my mates to be weird. And kind to me when I'm crying. *And* kind to worms.'

Kind when she was crying?

And *worms*?

Uh?

She blinked at me.

'Yeah – like that time right here, in this funny, little house . . .'

Her face went all straight. And then red. She started folding her cuff back on her coat, and then unfolding it again.

My brain slowly turned on.

Anna was the park girl? The crying, yellow-coat girl?

It suddenly made total sense.

That's how she'd known I was called William. And how to draw Gooner. And that's why she'd made a beeline for me that first morning at school.

Of course I hadn't realised it was her as she'd been so hidden inside that yellow coat. 'But , . . why didn't you *say* you knew me?' I said.

'Well, I nearly did. But then when you didn't recognise me, I thought we could have a fresh start,' she said, twizzling Gooner's ears. 'You know, delete the embarrassing bit where I wail at you, wearing my mum's horrid old coat.'

I looked at her, amazed.

Anna was *embarrassed?*

'But . . . you don't care what people think of you!' I said.

'Oh, I DO,' she said, her eyes widening. 'I was scared stiff about school. I didn't sleep at all the night before. So I was so glad when you let me go round with you.'

LET ME?

'But you just seem so confident . . .' I said.

'All an act,' she said. Then, in a gritted-teeth whisper, 'Like, I'm completely TERRIFIED about tonight. Mr Withington asked me to be in the show too, but . . .' She grabbed my arm. 'Oh, Will – please come and be in the show with me. We can help each other. Don't make me do it by myself!'

I tugged my hands through my hair, trying to catch up.

So . . .

Anna liked me BECAUSE I was weird and kind to worms.

She liked me *WITHOUT* my charm.

And now she was telling me she was as scared about doing the show as I was.

I'd really understood nothing, had I?

Nothing.

'Okay,' I heard myself say. 'We'll do it together.'

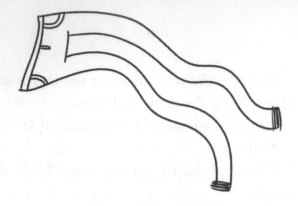

Chapter 34

Time was getting on.

I promised I'd meet them at school in forty-five minutes – Anna had invited Lu to come and watch too. I went home to change.

And face Mum.

I crept in the back door and into the hall.

The door of the Snog was half-open, and I could hear Mum and Shaun in there.

But not snogging.

Arguing.

I couldn't believe my ears.

Or rather, *Mum* was arguing. Shaun was being

218

calm. And Mum had definitely stopped pretending to be all sugary in front of him now. She was being really uppity – and moaning all about me.

'WHERE is he? I don't know what's going on with him! Do you know Gooner threw up this morning – and it was QUITE clear that Woody had fed him his packed lunch. What is he even eating at school?'

Oops . . .

'Well, he's only just started there,' said Shaun. 'It's a big transition, and he's sensitive. It's a lot to deal with, that's all.'

Mum sighed. 'Well, if he doesn't turn up soon, he'll be letting people down tonight. Ducking out at the last minute – I don't like that! And it'll be *good* for him to do this show – he needs to push himself and find some grit now he's at secondary, or he'll get walked all over.'

Yeah, like I didn't get walked over at primary, Mum! But I'd never told her about Della and Casey. I couldn't trust her not to go bowling up at school and making a big motor-mouth fuss, which would've made everything so much worse.

There was a pause.

Then Shaun said quietly: 'He's different to you, Suze. Maybe it'd be better just to let him choose for himself whether he does this show.'

Wow, Shaun.

He was standing up to Mum. Saying what he thought.

And I'd thought he was a wuss . . .

He got it full blast then.

'ACTUALLY, Shaun, I think this is for me to decide, don't you?' snapped Mum, turning up her volume.

I could hear noises like someone getting off the sofa. I reckoned Mum was about to flounce out in a strop. So I nipped inside the downstairs loo out of sight, just ducking my head in time before I crashed into Mum's bamboo wind-chime thing, which would've so given my game away.

I kept the loo door open a bit so I could still hear them.

But Mum didn't come out, because Shaun hadn't finished with her.

'Well, obviously you're the parent, and I don't want to interfere,' he said, matter-of-factly. 'But I live here now too. And what I see is that you need to back off, Suze. He's growing up and he needs to find his own way.'

Well, it was quite a speech. And he really seemed to GET me too. He understood stuff *much* more than Mum.

I'd been wrong about him too.

So wrong . . .

My throat choked up again.

Shaun was saying all this to Mum in her berserk-bull mode. He was sticking his neck out.

And he was doing it for ME.

Chapter 35

I hid behind the loo door as Mum came bundling out of the Snog, blotchy-faced, and into the kitchen.

Shaun didn't follow her.

And in that moment, everything switched around in my head.

I didn't want Mum and Shaun to fight. Because now more than anything, I *didn't* want Shaun to leave.

What could I do? I crept out of the loo just as Shaun came shuffling out into the hall too.

He jumped when he saw me, and then nodded

hello. I could tell he knew I'd heard everything.

'Thanks,' I whispered. And he nodded and smiled, holding his palms up, like: *well, I tried.*

I pointed to the kitchen to tell him I was going to talk to Mum. Even though I had no idea what I was going to say to her.

He understood, and shuffled back into the Snog, out of the way.

I crept up to the kitchen door. Mum was sitting at the table with her head in her hands, sniffing, with wet tissues scattered all around her. I took a deep breath and went in.

'Hi, Mum.'

She sat bolt upright.

'Oh. Woods, you're back. I . . . '

I knew half of her wanted to give me a rollicking for being late, but it was like all the energy had drained out of her. She stayed silent, looking down at the tissue she was fiddling with.

'I've been home a while, actually,' I said. 'And I couldn't help hearing you and Shaun.'

She nodded, screwing the tissue tighter into her hand.

'I know he's right . . .' she began, still not looking at me.

'Yeah, I reckon he is, Mum.' My voice had gone deep and strange. Seeing anyone cry usually made me cry too, but especially Mum. I swallowed to try and unchoke my throat. 'I know you're my mum, and I still have to listen to you. But I'm nearly twelve, and I just want to make my own lunch now.'

Why had I picked on *lunch*? It wasn't at all the main thing, even though it drove me nuts.

'And also . . . I wanna choose my own clothes. And shoes . . . and bag,' I went on, warming up to it.

Basically STOP making me weird, Mum!

I'd worked out that I was stuck with weirdness – and even my new friends didn't seem to mind. But it had to be MY kind of weird. Not hers.

I sat down at the table next to her. She was still nodding slowly.

'I do see that,' she said. 'It's just hard not to boss you – you've always been so unsure of yourself. Like your dad, I s'pose – all his swagger was just a big front. He was terribly insecure underneath too.'

Dad?

Is that *right*?

Oh.

Is that why he'd never go anywhere without his charm – like Nan said?

Mum arranged some pens in a line on the tablecloth, biting her lip. 'And I'm sure not having a dad around didn't help you either . . . '

'Yeah, well, I've kind of got him back recently,' I said. 'Nan's showed me loads of pictures and told me some things.'

Mum put her hand on mine, looking at me, soft-eyed.

'Good-looking lad, wasn't he?' she sighed. 'Listen, I know I knock him – and he was a pain in the neck, a stupid show-off, and really let us down! But he could be all right sometimes, your dad. For one thing, he loved animals like you. He was a strict vegetarian – we always agreed on that, at least.'

My dad was a veggie?

Uh? That couldn't be right?!

'But Nan told me he loved burgers!'

Mum laughed.

'There was a lot Barbie didn't know about her perfect son, I can tell you. But she's such a force, that he just pretended to agree with her for an easy life – and then did his own thing behind her back.'

I pressed my lips together. Well, that sounded familiar!

'So he didn't eat meat burgers *at all*?' I asked.

She shook her head. 'Your nan thought growing boys needed red meat, and she wouldn't be told otherwise. She kept on cooking him steak – but he just stuffed it all in his napkin, and gave it to his old dog later.'

She grinned.

Mum was actually *grinning* about my dad!

'Yeah, Barbie seems soft, but she's pretty much the Iron Lady in pink,' she went on. 'Which is why when you started seeing her, I was afraid she'd try and take over YOU too. And sure enough, she wasted no time. Buying you a pile of stuff. And those awful cakes!'

It was true in one way. Nan could be so in-your-face.

But I knew something else was true too.

'Actually I think Nan likes seeing me, cos she's still so sad,' I said gently. 'Because . . . well . . . yeah, you just have to imagine . . .'

Mum looked up at me sharply, like I'd slapped her. Her eyes filled and she did a shrug and a nod. A bit sheepish.

And it suddenly seemed the moment to ask her something I'd been wondering about. Seeing she wasn't hating on Dad and Nan quite so much right now.

'Mum . . . did Dad ever look *after* me?' Immediately my throat tightened and I had to gulp.

Mum got up and went to the dresser, and came back with an old, scuffed envelope I'd never seen before. She handed it to me without a word.

Inside was a single photo. A picture of Dad holding a baby.

Holding me. I was maybe about one or two, and I was sitting in his strong arms, hugging his neck. We were both smiling our heads off.

I couldn't stop looking at it. It had made me go all zingy from head to foot.

'He didn't change any nappies, but he did play with you for hours,' said Mum. 'He blew raspberries, and you'd pull his face around and laugh.'

Ha! Dad'd played Mr Potato Head with me!

More tears were coming. I should've been all cried out by now, but instead my face was awash again.

'That photo was taken just before he went off to the US, travelling. The fateful trip,' said Mum with a big sigh. 'I expect your nan has plenty of other photos like it.'

I nodded. I'd ask Nan. Maybe they were somewhere in one of her forty-seven million photo albums.

Shaun stuck his head in, and ducked out again.

'It's okay, Shauny,' said Mum, calling him. 'You can come in now.' She reached out for his hand, and he shuffled in and gave her a hug

Good. They were friends again.

I suddenly looked at the clock.

It was time for the show *already*? In fact, I was going to be late unless I hurried . . .

Oh NO.

Why had I agreed? But I HAD agreed, so –

I wiped my damp face on a tea towel and took a deep breath.

'I *am* actually doing that New Parents' Evening show, Mum. You coming?'

'Blimey!' said Mum. '*Really?*'

My stomach was turning like a washing machine, but I nodded.

Then I wanted to laugh at her surprised face. *Mum* was actually lost for words.

I was sure that hadn't happened since 1981.

Chapter 36

I ran upstairs to change cos I was still wet from wandering about town in the rain.

I rummaged in a pile of stuff on my chair. What could I wear?

I threw my granny jumper on the floor – NOT that. And not my new, tight jeans and T-shirts either. I'd leave that level of coolness to Josh now.

In the end, I tugged on my old jogging bottoms and a jumper from Nan, and then my sheeps'-food-splodged jacket.

I glanced in the mirror.

I looked okay – like, not too weird, but not too cool.

In the middle. I would do.

I stuffed my biggest Rubik's Cube into my rucksack. I was going to need THAT. Then I hopped down the stairs, my heart thumping.

'Bye,' I called as I opened the front door. 'I'm going on ahead now – see you there!'

Cos if I was *actually* going to do this, there was something I needed to do before.

I flew through the puddles, being buffeted by the wind, feeling oddly excited. I felt like I'd had too much sugar or something.

I got to the graveyard. It was lit by some street lamps, but it was still quite dark. I should've been scared, but I wasn't. Kneeling down, I reached into my pocket and sprinkled the broken bits of the charm on to the grave.

'I broke the charm, Dad – and I'm so sorry,' I whispered. 'But do you know what? My friends still like me without it! And I have an idea yours would've too.'

I laughed then. It was either that or cry.

'But now I've got to rush off to do a *show*. I don't have the charm, but I still need your help – I still need you *with me*. So I'm going to bring you in my head . . . okay? And I'm going to do it for YOU, Dad!'

I hugged Dad's headstone, and ran.

Chapter 37

I was a bit late. The hall was already packed with parents and kids.

My stomach tightened as I looked around. Now I *really* wanted to chicken out again.

But Mr Withington saw me and hurried over.

'Aha! Glad you made it, Will,' he said. 'So, you ready for our big moment?'

'Um . . .'

NO!

'Er, yes, sir,' I muttered.

'We're going to be great . . . or rather YOU are,' Mr Withington said. 'I've been practising with my cube, but I was never any good. Expect to wipe the floor with me.'

More like I'm expecting to wipe the floor with my whole body, I thought, when I faint on stage.

But I just nodded again.

Get a grip, Woods – you're doing it for Dad, remember!

'We're starting in two minutes. Those chairs at the front are for the performers,' he said, pointing.

Anna was there already, beckoning to me and mouthing that she'd saved me a seat. I made my way towards her.

I spotted Lu in the crowd – sitting with Mum and Shaun!

And Josh was there too – in the performers' chairs.

I felt my face redden up as I reached him.

Hi Josh – yep, it's me, Crying Boy . . .

But he beamed.

'All right, mate?' He fist-bumped me as I went past.

Seemed he still liked me too . . .

Me without my charm.

Just me.

I nodded and smiled back at him.

Maybe I'd thank him later for sending Anna and Lu to find me.

Anna gripped my arm as I sat down.

'I thought you'd deserted me!' she hissed.

I shook my head, and started to apologise, but the head had walked on stage.

'Welcome, everyone!'

As the head talked, Anna gripped my arm tighter and tighter until I thought my arm was going to fall off.

I felt sick, but I kept my mind on Dad. Thinking about how he would've been in shows in this same hall.

THIS SAME HALL.

Anna was first up.

And she needn't have worried – she was *amazing*. You'd never have guessed she was nervous. She was like a singer off the telly. Not one of those dim ones who dance about in a bra – just one that was *brilliant* at singing.

The audience clapped her loads, especially me.

Then some other kids had their turns, including Josh, who did all this mad parkour – handstands and somersaults in the air, all sorts.

And then it was my turn.

When the head said my name I kind of jumped, and my stomach clenched hard.

'Now for a Rubik's Cube race! Pupil versus teacher too, so it could get heated! Mr Withington – are you ready?'

Mr Withington stepped onto the stage with his cube, pretending to loosen up his muscles, for a joke. Everyone giggled.

But I still hadn't moved. All MY muscles had locked up.

Anna sort of shoved me to my feet.

'Just breathe,' she whispered

I nodded, shook myself into life, and strode to the front stiffly.

I stood next to Mr Withington in a bright spotlight, which was making me blink and squint.

My arms were clamped to my sides, and the walls were closing in on me.

Stay upright!

All those eyes . . .

All those parents . . . *Dad* would've been out there with them too.

Should've been. If it hadn't happened to him.

But he *was* here – in my head.

Heart.

I gulped and took some deep breaths like Anna had told me to, and wiped my hands on my trousers.

'Ready?'

The head looked back and forth between me and Mr Withington. 'Set . . . GO!'

My brain was still panicking, but my fingers didn't care – they knew what to do. They were doing the cube by themselves, turning it round, twisting it this way and that.

It was just me and my Rubik's now. I wasn't looking at Mr Withington.

Red.

Green.

Blue.

And . . . DONE!

I held the cube high in the air, breathing hard.

All the sides were the same.

Everyone clapped, and Anna whooped.

Mr Withington held his cube up – he'd hardly begun it.

He hung his head, and everyone laughed.

'I declare a winner!' called the head. 'Now that was FAST. Maybe a new world record?'

Of course it wasn't – and I could do it faster.

But I'd done it.

I'd done it for Dad.

I'd kept my promise.

Chapter 38

The show finished soon after.

'Woody!' Mum cried, rushing over and hugging me.

Shaun winked at me and mouthed: *good job*!

I was out in public with them. Mum was hugging me AT SCHOOL. But for once I could just about deal with it.

Lu came over too.

'YEAHHHHHH!' she grinned. 'You got dem skills, bro!'

'Thanks!' I said, smiling. 'Phew!'

Mr Withington was stacking chairs, and waved me over.

'Hey, Will! You totally thrashed me! I can't show my face.' Then he gave me a thumbs-up. 'Nah, really – you did great. Thanks for helping me out. I see you don't exactly have your dad's love of centre-stage, but you did it.'

I smiled and nodded. He wasn't wrong about the stage thing . . .

I turned and spotted Josh across the hall, walking on his hands while a group of kids watched him. Now there was another boy who loved the centre-stage.

Maybe Dad had been like that.

I wandered over.

Two girls swept by arm in arm. Kendall and one of her Girls-A-Very-Loud.

'We liked your moves, Josh,' Kendall's friend called out.

'Why, thank you!' Josh did a big bow, and they laughed.

Hey, that was the way to deal with it.

'Will was good too, wasn't he, Kendy,' said

her friend, nudging her. Kendall nodded and smiled at me shyly. Still liking me . . .

And then – I don't know what happened to me, but I suddenly found myself bowing low too.

'Thank you!'

The girls giggled again, and hurried off across the hall.

I'd done 'a Josh' . . .

Or maybe I'd done 'a Dad'.

Either way it was SO MUCH better than my usual red-faced mumbling.

And, with everyone still liking me so much, it looked like I'd have to learn *new* ways to cope with it.

Chapter 39

I told Mum I was going to walk home with my friends.

We piled outside the school hall into the windy darkness, all of us together – me, Anna, Lu . . . even Casey. Lu scowled at her, but Casey just looked blankly at her own feet, so Lu didn't say anything.

We were laughing at nothing. Especially Anna, who was the loudest laugher of all.

Josh was doing more parkour of course – he couldn't ever stay still – running along walls and climbing right up to the top of lamp posts.

Then me and him both hung off a street sign while Lu used my phone to take a picture.

'But DON'T prank my phone again!' I said to her sternly. She just laughed and stuck her tongue out at me.

'LET'S GET CHIPS!' yelled Anna, and we all cheered.

We searched our pockets for coins, and then raced each other down the road to the chip shop.

The chip shop was packed so Lu went into buy the chips while we waited outside.

'Lots of vinegar,' I called to Lu, through the window. I turned and – bang – the smile was wiped off my face. Because there, right in front of us, was Della.

I caught my breath.

I'd managed to avoid her for days, but my luck had just run out. She stopped dead. Our eyes met. And my whole body froze.

'Weirdy,' she sneered, curling her lip.

Then her eyebrows flew up.

'*Case?*' she said.

Casey turned round, saw Della, and sort of crumpled inside her coat on the spot. 'What are you doing, Case? Are you here with this lot? With *Weirdy*?'

Casey squirmed about, all hunched and big-eyed, and said nothing.

Della scowled. 'Come with me! Come NOW!'

Josh and Anna didn't know Della. They were chatting, and hadn't even noticed what was going on. And Lu was still in the chip shop.

Nope, this was mine.

I had to do something about this.

Me.

Once and for all.

'You can stay with us, Casey, if you like,' I said loudly, my belly quivering.

Anna and Josh looked round then, in surprise.

I stared at Della – right into her eyes. I could see she was totally taken aback, but she eyeballed me back furiously. I didn't look away – even though my heart was thundering, and my legs had gone tingly.

We kept our eyes locked for ages. Then Della

sort of spluttered. She opened her mouth and then closed it. She looked at me for another second, and then she looked away FIRST.

She began walking off, but then she turned back.

'Case – come with me NOW,' she ordered again, like Casey was her dog. Except I'd never talk to Gooner that horribly. 'You're my cousin – we're family. Come, or I'm telling Auntie Taz.'

Casey looked between Della and us with a pinched face, like she was being asked to walk the plank, and we were all Casey-eating crocodiles.

And then she went.

As they walked off, I could see Della muttering stuff to her and giving her right evils.

And I felt sorry for Casey. I honestly did.

'Blimey – WHO was that?' asked Anna.

'Della-salmonella,' I said, 'as Lu likes to call her. She likes to make people cry.'

'Right,' said Anna, making an ewww face.

'Was that DELLA?' asked Lu, appearing with two big trays of chips. 'Did I miss something?'

We all nodded at the same time. Then Anna elbowed me, grinning.

'But someone took her on. You won that stare-down good and proper!'

I had. I was amazed.

'Yeah, mate,' said Josh. 'That was awesome.'

He looked at me with serious eyes, like he really meant it. But it didn't last long. Because without warning, he threw himself into this springy flip along the pavement, surprising a lady on a bike so much she wobbled like mad, and we all fell about laughing.

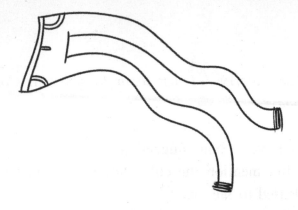

Chapter 40

I kept putting off telling Nan that I'd broken the charm. Even though I knew I'd have to tell her eventually.

On Saturday morning I'd started to dial her number four times, and then each time put the phone down again. In the end I decided to text it to her. Just the basics. Get it over and done with.

So sorry – I accidentally broke the cube charm. Please forgive me. W x

She replied in two seconds.

Don't worry – I just want to see you. Come today? x

So I went. Nan hugged me at the door, and didn't mention the cube. She just seemed very pleased to see me.

We sat on her sofa together. She'd got me some fizzy juice and one of those posh biscuit assortment tins.

I was starving so I ate three custard creams on the trot, trying not to make too many crumbs on her posh sofa. Then I reached for a different biscuit.

'Oh, wait!' she squealed. 'I think that kind have coconut in them!'

I stopped with the biscuit halfway to my mouth. Uh? So? I liked coconut.

'Will's allergic to coconut – it gave him a terrible tummy, poor baby.'

'But I'm not him,' I said, before I could stop myself. And maybe a bit too firmly.

Her eyes flew open like I'd given her an electric shock, and then instantly filled with tears. She scrabbled up her sleeve for a tissue and dabbed under her eyes. Then her hand went to her mouth – but it was trembling, and her long, red nails rattled against her teeth.

'Sorry,' I whispered.

'No, it's okay,' she said. 'You're right. It's just . . . *hard*. Still hard. And you're so much like him.'

'Yes, except . . . I'm me,' I said, quietly.

She nodded, her black eyelash make-up tracking down her cheeks in muddy, little streams.

'Do you know, I can't even go to the grave?' she said, in barely a whisper.

'Oh?' I said. 'But the grave looks so . . .'

She waved her hand in front of her face: 'I've always paid someone else to keep it neat. I'd rather that than go myself and get reminded that he's . . . isn't here any more. I like things that make me remember him being alive – like you!'

A tear plopped in a black droplet on to her pale skirt.

I leant forward and took her hand.

'If you *do* want to go, Nan, I'll come with you.'

She gave my hand a tight squeeze, and nodded. She even didn't tell me off for calling her Nan.

'Now?' I asked, softly.

Now was good. I might get too scared to go with her if I had time to think about it.

She hesitated and then nodded again.

So we went.

Right then and there.

We parked outside the church. I felt my belly tense as Nan did her hair in the mirror in a fluster. She had this tight, white face like she was forgetting to breathe.

We walked into the graveyard, arm in arm, without talking. The sky had gone orange behind the church.

Nan was holding the car keys and shaking so much the keys were jingling, but she didn't seem to notice. So I gently took them off her and held her hand tight.

We stood together by the grave.

I wanted to cry but I had to look after Nan. She was swaying slightly. Then she started stroking the top of the grave over and over, and tears came streaming down her face. She was clinging to my hand like I was the only thing stopping her from falling in the grave too.

We stayed for ages like that.

'Thank you. You're a very kind, brave boy,' she whispered, eventually. 'Your dad would've been proud of you. Very proud indeed.'

Her words caught me, and I had to swallow hard.

Because this time I believed her.

Chapter 41

Three weeks later on a Saturday it was my birthday, and I invited my friends around to mine. Anna and Josh – and of course, Lu and Kai.

I didn't invite Casey. I was trying not to leave her out at school, but inviting her to mine would've been a step way too far. And anyway, Lu said, there was nice, and then there was TOO nice, and if I invited Casey she'd throw ice cream at her.

It was basically the biggest number of friends I'd ever invited to my house – so everyone started calling it 'Woody's Party'.

Yeah, I'd gone back to being called just Woody again – it was far less complicated that way.

And look at me having a party! Even if it was only a sort-of one.

'It's so nice you've made some new friends at Hawthorn,' said Mum, all grins.

Thanks for sounding so surprised, Mum!

But she had a point. I hadn't made any new friends for years. I'd never bothered to talk to anyone at primary much, other than Lu. The charm had made me do it now – one way or another.

The Saturday of my sort-of party was dry and sunny, even though it was nearly October. Mum dressed extra-weirdly in huge, orange-balloon clown trousers and a spotty, raggedy sack thing as a top – WHYYY, Mum? Then she made lots of carrot sticks and a homemade lentil dip that looked like cow pat and no one was going to eat.

Shaun was much more helpful. He'd worked like mad to get his hobbity mud-hut pizza oven finished so we could have pizzas.

Anna arrived early and walked around the

house and garden cooing at Shaun's oven and at all Mum's crystals and candles indoors.

'I *love* your house!' she said. 'Mine is so *boring*.'

Then everyone else arrived all at once and gave me so many presents and cards I was nearly buried. I opened them in a tearing frenzy, with Gooner helping me to pull off the paper with his teeth. He loved that job.

The best present was a worm farm from Anna. Ha.

Shaun yelled down the garden that the oven was ready, so we all got going decorating our own pizzas with a ton of toppings, and slid them into the fire on a wooden paddle. Then we sat about on deck chairs stuffing our faces in the sun, with our ducks quacking around us. They were literally the nicest pizzas ever.

Kai fell completely in love with Anna. They sat on the rug for ages with Gooner, patting his fluffy tummy, which was too full of pizza crusts, and chatting.

'So what's your favourite animal, Kai?' Anna

asked. He put his head on one side, covered with tomato ear to ear, and thought.

'Tractor,' he said, seriously.

Anna burst out laughing, and then so did Kai. He was so delighted to have made a joke that he shouted TRACTOR over and over again, getting louder and louder, until Lu had to tell him to stop. But it was the best joke I'd heard since I was twelve.

Me and Josh sat together. I was showing him how to do a Rubik's Cube, and we were mucking around and kaboom-ing the school roof, which we could see through the gap in the trees. Then Shaun joined in and made the loudest KABOOM of all and made everyone laugh, even Mum. Except I actually didn't want the school to be demolished any more. It could stay standing now if it liked.

We were completely full after all the pizza, but Mum still came out with birthday cake. She carried it out with twelve lit candles, and everyone started singing.

It was a big, gooey one with bits of fudge on it – definitely not one Mum had made.

'Nan brought you this,' said Mum. 'She dropped it round earlier.' Then she looked right at me with soft eyes and smiled.

SMILED.

Of course, I welled up then.

I gulped and tried to blow out the candles, but I didn't have any puff cos I was too choked.

I tried again several times, but I just couldn't do it.

And it suddenly felt so funny. I started laughing at myself. Wiping away my tears on my sleeve and giggling helplessly.

That got everyone else going too – and in the end we were all laughing.

'It's no good – you'll have to help me,' I cried.

'Okay!' said Anna. 'One, two, three . . . go!'

And we blew my candles out together. Apart from Kai, who did a big, spitty raspberry in my face.

Acknowledgements

Huge thanks to my agent, James Catchpole, for all his support, good thoughts and brainpower. And thanks too to the whole Catchpole A team: Celia, Lucy and Mainie.

More thank yous to the lovely Piccadilly team – especially Emma, Georgia and Monique.

And big hugs to Poppy, Lola and Steve for all the things and more.

Dawn McNiff

Dawn was born in a blue house by the sea in Sussex. She now lives in a brown house in Gloucestershire with her two teenage daughters and lots of furry pets. In 2008 she did an MA in Writing for Young People at Bath Spa University, which was 100% fab. In the past, she has worked as a bereavement counsellor, a copywriter, a teaching assistant and a children's bookseller – but her best job has always been being a mummy. Dawn likes dancing to bad 80s songs, going for rainy walks, eating green soup, snoozing by her log-burner, and writing in cafes. (PS: Never challenge Dawn to a water fight cos you'll lose.) Follow Dawn on Twitter: @DawnMcNiff

ALSO BY DAWN McNIFF . . .

Little Celeste

Dawn McNiff

Friendship,
mischief, magic ...
It's written in the stars

A heart-warming tale about magic,
responsibility, mothers and daughters

A hilarious and heartfelt story for anyone
who just can't help worrying!

Piccadilly
P R E S S

Thank you for choosing a Piccadilly Press book.

If you would like to know more about our authors, our books or if you'd just like to know what we're up to, you can find us online.

www.piccadillypress.co.uk

You can also find us on:

We hope to see you soon!